DESERT CROSSING

Ned Butler had been hired by some folk to guide them across the desert known as the Cauldron, but then Jess Fuller put a bullet into Ned. Into this maelstrom came the renegade Link Hauser who tossed some dynamite into the works, and a mad miner. Before too long Link Hauser and his Gatling gun hit town and Lassiter wanted Hauser's blood. But what was the real reason for the trip across the desert?

H. H. CODY

DESERT CROSSING

Complete and Unabridged

LINFORD
Leicester

First published in Great Britain in 2007 by
Robert Hale Limited
London

First Linford Edition
published 2008
by arrangement with
Robert Hale Limited
London

British Library CIP Data

Cody, H. H.
   Desert crossing.—Large print ed.—
   Linford western library
   1. Western stories
   2. Large type books
   I. Title
   823.9'14 [F]

ISBN 978–1–84782–203–1

Published by
F. A. Thorpe (Publishing)
Anstey, Leicestershire

Set by Words & Graphics Ltd.
Anstey, Leicestershire
Printed and bound in Great Britain by
T. J. International Ltd., Padstow, Cornwall

This book is printed on acid-free paper

1

'Sure is a hot one,' Jim Crowe said, wiping the sweat from his leathery face, and looking out over the Cauldron.

'Want another?' Rafe Lassiter asked him, bending to take the glass from his partner's hand.

'Thought you'd never ask,' Crowe said, licking his thin lips.

Lassiter picked up the glass, and looked down the trail out of town.

'You see somethin'?' Crowe asked him, putting his hands on the rims of the wheelchair, and forcing himself up to see what Lassiter was looking at.

'Stage is comin' in,' he replied, narrowing his eyes against the glare of the desert sun.

'What's so special about that?' Crowe asked, lowering himself into the chair. 'Comes through every couple of days.'

'Not with an escort of blue bellies,

an' Mitch whipping the team like Ol' Nick himself was after him.'

Crowe put his hand to his eyes again. 'Maybe Ol' Nick is after him.'

Lassiter went into the dark of the saloon, and put the glasses on the bar top.

'Two more Herve,' he said to the barkeep.

Behind him reflected in the mirror, he could see Ned Butler, and a couple of other fellas playing poker with a deck of sweat-stained cards.

'Yer amigo has got a thirst on him today,' Herve said, putting the two glasses on the bar top.

'Sure has,' Lassiter said, non-commitally.

He didn't want to get into a discussion about Crowe's drinking habits or anything else. Crowe had been marked by the Grim Reaper, but he was going to make the fella wait until he was ready, and if he wanted a few beers, so what? It was a harmless enough thing.

Lassiter pushed through the batwings, and handed the glass to Crowe.

'Thanks.' Crowe grinned.

The stage had come an appreciable way since Lassiter had gone into the saloon. The desert dust was churning up thick and fast.

'Sure givin' them horses a beatin',' Lassiter mused, putting the glass to his lips. 'Gonna be lucky if they live long enough to git a drink.'

A couple of fellas came out into the street to watch the stage.

'Hi, Driscol,' Lassiter said to the owner of the boarding house where they were staying.

''Mornin', Rafe,' Driscol answered, following Lassiter's gaze in the direction of the stage.

'We were wonderin' that ourselves,' Lassiter said, reading Driscol's mind.

As Lassiter spoke, a tall fair-haired fella came out of Driscol's place and went into the saloon without looking at any of them.

'Who's the tight-mouthed fella?' Lassiter asked Driscol when the fella had gone into the Last Drop, the batwings creaking behind him.

'Goes by the name of Jess Fuller. Got in late last night. Been askin' about your buddy Ned Butler.'

'He's gonna find him in there,' Lassiter said, taking a pull from his glass.

The stage was coming into town, just passing the livery stable, and the general store. The troopers riding beside it looked as tired as the team pulling the coach. As they hauled up outside the Wells Fargo Office, Lassiter saw Mitch kick on the brake and pull on the leathers. Straightaway, the team dropped their heads, and pawed at the hard ground, sweat coming out of their bodies like steam coming out of a railway engine.

Lassiter watched as Mitch climbed off the stage, pulled off his hat, and wiped his forehead. Jacko Jackson, the shotgun, tossed the mailbag down, and then reached behind for a travelling bag that had been strapped to the roof of the stage.

Captain Stranks had dismounted, and was opening the door.

A comely young woman got out of the dust-covered coach and spoke to Captain Stranks. Lassiter watched as the argument started up, then the woman picked up her bag and headed for Driscol's. Mitch and Stranks looked at each other, but just shrugged.

Stranks said something to the sergeant, and the sergeant led the troop down the street to where they could let their horses rest before they watered them.

Stranks looked in Lassiter's direction and came across to him.

'Nice to see you, Stranks,' Lassiter said to the captain.

'Nice to see you Rafe, Jim,' he said, wiping his face with his bandanna.

'The lady that important that she needs an escort?' Lassiter asked Stranks.

Stranks smiled ruefully. 'It ain't her, it's Link Hauser. He's on the loose in the territory, and worst of all he got lucky.'

'How's that?' Crowe asked.

'One of our boys deserted, and took a Gatling with him, and a wagonload of ammunition.'

Crowe whistled. Lassiter looked worried.

'Got any notion where he is?' Lassiter asked Captain Stranks.

Stranks shrugged and jerked his finger over his shoulder. 'Take your pick.'

'Plenty to choose from. Except, he won't be goin' into the Cauldron,' Lassiter opined.

Stranks said nothing. 'I'd best be getting back to my men.'

Lassiter and Crowe watched him head to where his men were resting the horses.

'Could be hell to pay,' Crowe said.

'Sure could,' Lassiter replied, finishing his beer.

As he put the empty glass on the rail the sound of a shot came from the inside of the Last Drop. Lassiter and Crowe turned to each other as the stranger came hurrying through the batwing doors, and headed for the horse tethered outside the boarding house. For a few seconds Lassiter watched him, then went into the saloon.

Everybody was crowded round the body on the floor. Lassiter looked round for Ned Butler, then he realized that Ned was on the floor. Those gathered round Ned made way for Lassiter.

Ned was lying among a heap of cards, some poker chips, blood already staining his chest.

Lassiter got up, and looked at Herve. 'What happened?'

'Fella came into the saloon an' asked if he could join the game. Don't think Ned was too happy, but the fella joined. After a while, Ned started winnin' for the first time, then the fella said Ned was cheatin', called him, an' just shot him down.'

'No, I can't see Ned cheatin'. He wasn't the sort,' Lassiter said. 'Somebody get Sheriff Donaldson.'

Herve went through the batwing doors.

Lassiter looked down at Ned Butler. Ned had taken him across the Cauldron a couple of times, and shown him the underground water supplies that only he and the Indians knew. Ned Butler was the last fella that would have cheated another man out of a cent.

Lassiter went through the batwing doors. He could see the beefy Sheriff Ike Donaldson hurrying up the street towards the saloon. Crowe was watching him too.

'See which way the fella went that came out of here?' he asked Crowe.

Crowe turned in his direction. 'Was it him that done the shootin'?'

'Shot Ned Butler,' Lassiter said evenly.

Crowe's eyes hardened. 'Shot Ned? What did he do a crazy thing like that for? Ned was a harmless enough man.'

'That fella didn't seem to think so,' Lassiter said as Donaldson came onto the veranda.

'What's bin goin' on? Herve says Ned Butler's bin shot.'

'He's inside,' Lassiter pushed the batwing aside to let the sheriff in. Donaldson took out his handkerchief, and pushed back his hat, as he started to mop his face.

'Where's the fella that done it?' he asked, gasping for the air.

'Rode out into the Cauldron,' Crowe said.

'What he do a fool thing like that for?' Donaldson asked them.

'He said Ned was cheatin' at poker,' Lassiter told him.

'I mean what's he doin' goin' up into the Cauldron? Must be crazy,' Donaldson went on.

'Crazy or not, that's where he went,' Lassiter said patiently.

Donaldson said, 'Git the undertaker up here. Otherwise Ned'll be stinkin' worse than usual.'

Herve went out into the street again.

'What about the fella that did this?' Lassiter said, pointing to Ned, who was picking up a fine collection of flies.

He bent and flapped his hand. The

flies pulled away from Ned's body.

'Go up into the Cauldron? Yer as crazy as him that did this,' Donaldson said, wiping his face again.

'You mean yer just gonna let him get away with this?' Lassiter said angrily.

'Come on, Rafe,' Donaldson said. 'Where's he gonna go with one horse, an' one canteen of water?'

'Then why did he go up there?' Lassiter asked.

Donaldson shook his head. 'Dunno.'

'You gonna git up a posse?' Lassiter asked as Herve came back leading Dan Bradbury, the undertaker.

'You any idea how many folks there are in this town that would ride up into the Cauldron after that fella?'

Lassiter knew that the answer was none.

'Get a couple of fellas to carry Ned over to my parlour,' Dan Bradbury said.

2

Jess Fuller had headed out into the Cauldron just as fast as his horse could carry him. He kept going for a couple of hours, and finally hauled on the leathers and brought his horse to a stop near a stand of rocks. He guided his horse up the narrow gully until it widened out into a flat, rocky bowl.

In the shelter of an overhang, his spare horse grazed patiently on the stunted grass. It nickered and raised its head as he approached. Fuller dismounted, and walked cautiously towards it.

His soothing words belied the ruthless killer who had shot Ned Butler in the heart. When he had settled it, he moved over to a patch of loose soil. He started to scrape out the soil until he came to the two waterskins that he had buried the previous day. He pulled them out, and shook the sand off them.

Fuller opened up a waterskin, and took a drink, then he gave one to the horses. For a moment, he sat giving himself some rest. When he was ready, he went back to the hole he had opened up, and pulled out a couple of sacks of provisions. He made himself a frugal meal, and looked round. He reckoned he was safe for a while. When the hot day had drifted on another hour, he mounted the horse he had rode in on, and went in the direction of Spanish Wells, after hitching the spare horse to his pommel.

As he rode he thought about Hank Stirling, and the information he had reluctantly given him. Stirling was made of tougher stuff than Fuller had thought. It had been a full day of sweating and working with his knife before Stirling had told him where Jack Whelan had run to when he had run out on the gang with the gold from the railway robbery.

Spanish Wells, a fair-sized town, was just beyond the Mexican side of the border. Stirling couldn't help him with exactly where the gold was, but Spanish Wells and Jack Whelan were a good place to start from. The only other flies in the desert ointment were Whelan's wife, Jennifer, and the fella she was riding with, Jim Trantor. He had been Whelan's right hand, but Whelan had left him on the trail with a bullet in him so the law could pick him up. But Jennifer Whelan had other ideas. She had got Trantor away before the law could get its hands on him.

The robbery had worked out just fine, and everything was going smooth as water down a thirsty man's throat, until Jack had got greedy and stupid, and decided to cut the rest of the gang out of the deal. The part of the deal where everybody got rich. Stupid bastard.

★　★　★

Lassiter had gone outside to speak to Crowe. 'Donaldson isn't gonna be goin'

13

after that killer,' he said.

Crowe shrugged. 'Don't surprise me none. Ain't the most energetic man you could meet. The .45s he wears, they're just Sunday-wearing guns. God help this town if some real bad fellas come rollin' through.'

For a minute Lassiter said nothing, he just thought them bad fellas might be Link Hauser and his men.

'We're gonna be needin' some money pretty soon,' he said to Crowe. 'That last set of reward money's havin' to go pretty far.'

He knew that Crowe wouldn't like him talking about the last bounty they'd picked up. Crowe had collected a heap of buckshot in the legs that put him in the wheelchair, and the effects of the wound were slowly killing him, but he figured that Crowe already knew that.

'Figured it would be,' Crowe said suddenly, emptying the glass of beer he had been drinking from. 'What are we gonna do about it?'

Lassiter flinched. What was he going

to do about it, was what Crowe meant, but he wouldn't have said it.

'Might just take off after Hauser,' he said, hoping that Crowe wouldn't detect the seriousness in his voice.

'Go after Hauser?' Crowe asked him.

'Stranks said Hauser's got his hands on a Gatling gun an' a wagonload of ammunition. Must be worth somethin',' Lassiter said.

'Where are you gonna start lookin'?' Crowe asked, fidgeting with the beer glass.

Captain Stranks had taken his detail off in the opposite direction to the Cauldron, but the way Lassiter figured it there were a few small settlements over in the Cauldron, and Hauser might just take it into his head to risk it and cross the wasteland. There wasn't much law up there, and no army.

'Seems like yer thinkin' on it,' Crowe said.

'Maybe I am,' Lassiter replied when he took the glass off Crowe. 'I'll get you another drink.'

'Thanks,' Crowe said.

As Lassiter was pushing his way through the doors, four fellas were carrying Ned Butler out on an old door.

'Two more beers,' he said to Herve, putting the coins on the bar.

Herve went and pulled the beers. Lassiter looked out of the window while he was waiting for Herve to come back with the beers. A rider came in from the opposite direction to the Cauldron. He looked hot and beat. Lassiter watched as he spoke to the town bum who pointed to Driscol's boarding house. The fella gigged his horse in that direction, got out of the saddle, and went inside.

Lassiter lost interest and went to the bar, where Herve was putting the beers up.

'Got a stranger in town,' Crowe said as Lassiter passed him his drink.

'I saw,' Lassiter replied, looking at the boarding house.

'Want a bite to eat?' Lassiter asked Crowe.

Crowe thought about it, then said, 'Not right now.'

'I'm goin' down to the cafe fer a bite,' Lassiter said, finishing his beer.

He put the glass on the floor beside Crowe and headed for the little Mexican cafe. The place was empty, but he had to wait for the man that owned it to come out from the back, and take his order.

When the tortillas came, he went and sat at the back where he could see anybody that came in. The food filled him up, and he dropped the payment on the table and headed for the door.

Halfway up the street the sound of a muffled drum caused him to stop.

He turned round, and saw a hearse pulled by a couple of sweating blacks with plumes on their heads hauling Ned up to Boot Hill. Lassiter pulled off his hat, and waited for the hearse to pass. There were no mourners. He figured he'd end that way, being hauled up an empty street in a hearse with no mourners. The hearse passed, and he put on his hat, and went over to the Last Drop.

Crowe was sitting, his hat in his hand, when Lassiter got there. Driscol was with him. They all watched as Ned Butler went up the hill just outside Desert Wells. The horses toiled slowly, and the woman's voice came as a surprise.

'Have any of you fellas seen Ned Butler?' she asked quietly.

Lassiter turned and saw that it was the woman who had got off the stage.

'He's up there,' Driscol said.

The woman glanced in the direction of Boot Hill. 'I can't see Ned Butler.'

Driscol guffawed. 'That's because he's in the box in the hearse.'

Lassiter saw the anger cross her face. 'Damn, he's supposed to be taking me across the Cauldron.'

'Guess he changed his mind,' Driscol said, with a loud, coarse laugh.

'Damn Ned Butler and his change of mind,' she snapped at Driscol.

'Ned didn't mean to get shot,' Crowe said.

'Shot?' the woman calmed down a mite.

Crowe looked up at her. 'Yeah, some fella said Ned was cheatin' at cards, an' shot him for it, then he went riding into the Cauldron, which makes even less sense than accusin' Ned of cheatin' at cards.'

'What did this fella look like?' she asked Crowe.

Crowe told her, and Lassiter watched some of the colour drain from her face.

'Seems like yer gonna have to get somebody else to take you over the Cauldron.' Driscol told her.

'Thanks for the advice,' she told Driscol, and turned and hurried back to the boarding house.

'Wonder why she wanted to go over the Cauldron?' Driscol mused.

Lassiter had asked himself the same question.

He pondered things for a while, then said to Crowe when the others had gone, 'This could be a way of making that *dinero* we're gettin' short of.'

'More than likely,' Crowe ruminated. 'Could say it was meant to be. Why don't you go an' see her?'

'Just what I was thinkin',' Lassiter replied.

A few minutes later, he followed the woman across the street.

'First floor back,' Driscol told him. 'Right next to you an' yer drunken sidekick.'

Lassiter half-turned back, but realized it wasn't worth it.

The inside of the boarding house was dark, hot, and smelled of the desert.

He found the room, and knocked hard on the door. When it was opened, he recognized the stranger who had ridden in earlier.

'What do you want?' the stranger asked in an unfriendly voice.

'The woman who came in here a couple of minutes ago said she wanted a guide across the Cauldron.'

'So?' was the brusque answer.

Lassiter wanted to hit the man in the mouth. 'I know the Cauldron well enough to get her across, if she still wants to get across.'

'Wait here,' the fella said, and went inside.

Lassiter waited until he came back. 'We still want to get across the Cauldron. Come in an' see the lady.'

Lassiter followed him in, and heard the door close behind him.

The woman was sitting on the chair near the window.

'He says you know the Cauldron well enough to be able to get us across it,' she said.

'I know it that well,' Lassiter told her. 'Gotta tell you though, the Cauldron ain't no place for a woman this time of the year, so unless you've got pressin' business in Spanish Wells, go someplace else.'

'My husband ain't someplace else, he's in Spanish Wells with a bullet in him: that's why I've got to get over there. I hired Ned Butler to do the job but, like your friends said, he got himself shot.'

'S'pose Ned Butler knew yer name,' Lassiter said.

'Sure he knew our names,' the fella interrupted.

'Take it easy, Jim,' she said to him. 'You're right. I'm Jennifer Whelan, this is Jim Trantor.'

'I'm Rafe Lassiter,' he said. 'How much did you pay Ned for his services?'

'We would have paid him two hundred dollars,' she said, reaching for her bag.

'OK, two hundred it is,' Lassiter said. 'We start at half past five in the mornin'.'

'What's wrong with startin' now?' Trantor put in.

''Cos it's too late in the day. It's gonna be over a hundred by the middle of the day. That's too damn hot to travel. You got a horse?' he said to Jennifer.

'No.'

'I'll get you one and a packhorse for the extra water and food. I'll need fifty dollars, for the supplies.'

She opened the bag and took out a wad of money. She passed it to him.

'OK. I'll be outside the livery stable in the mornin'. See you then.'

Lassiter went over to the saloon where Crowe was still sitting sipping at his beer.

'I'm gonna be takin' them across the Cauldron. We're gonna be startin' at first light. Got the money too,' he told Crowe.

'You'd best be gettin' over to Driscol's an' gettin' the stuff packed,' Crowe said, finishing his beer.

They got over to Driscol's, and Lassiter took out the two hundred that Jennifer Whelan had given him.

Lassiter peeled off fifty dollars, and gave them to Crowe.

'This will settle with Driscol. It'll leave some for you to get some grub, an' medicine, but it won't leave you enough to get Driscol's kid to go to the saloon to get you some redeye,' Lassiter said.

'Hell Rafe, how'd you know about that? It was just the once. An' you know it helps with the pain,' Crowe said, without any trace of whining or self-pity in his voice.

'I know that Crowe, but it ain't right you sendin' kids fer yer redeye,' Lassiter said as he started to clean his gun. He had tossed his rig on the bed, along with his last box of shells.

He wasn't happy at the idea of leaving Crowe, but they needed the money the job would bring in, and he knew they would never go collecting bounty together again.

He cleaned his stuff in silence, then said to Crowe, 'I'm gonna go to the livery to buy a couple of horses.'

'See you later,' Crowe said.

He listened to Lassiter's boots echoing along the passage, and then he reached under his bed to take out the bottle of redeye that Driscol's kid had got for him. He pulled the cork, and put it to his lips. The first redeye of the morning sure tasted the best. He belched loudly, and put it back under his bed.

★　★　★

Out on a rock stack that overlooked Desert Wells, one of Link Hauser's scouts was folding up the U.S. Army issue field glasses, and put them in his saddlebag. Climbing into the saddle he headed for Hauser's camp a couple of miles away.

'The army pulled out a couple of hours ago,' he told Hauser. 'An' they went in the wrong direction.'

Hauser laughed noisily, his blackened teeth showing as he laughed. Link Hauser was a big fella, who carried two army Colts stuck in his belt that he had taken from the stiffening bodies of a couple of cavalry troopers, along with a hunting knife, which he used to get any information he wanted from anybody who might have it.

'Git yerself a drink, an' some grub,' he said to his scout. 'We'll go an' pay them a visit tomorrow just to shake them lazy asses out of their comfortable beds.'

The scout went off to get his drink and his grub.

3

Lassiter was the first to the livery the following morning. Jennifer and Trantor came along a few minutes later.

Lassiter knocked on the door of the livery, and waited until the owner got it opened. Once they were inside, he tossed him some coins and started saddling the horse he had bought for the woman. Trantor started saddling his own. When Lassiter had finished, he saddled his horse, and then the packhorse. The horse moved nervously as he put on the waterskins and the extra food. He patted its rump.

'You about ready?' he asked her, when he had finished with the packhorse.

'Yeah,' she replied.

'You ready?' he asked Trantor, who was looking like he had a hard night in the saloon.

'I'm ready,' he said. His voice was

thick and dry, confirming Lassiter's suspicions that he had been drinking the night before.

'Hope you ain't brought any liquor along with you. Ain't no place fer it in the desert.'

'I'll be just fine,' Trantor replied. 'You just make sure you're OK.'

Lassiter wondered how much trouble he was going to cause when the sun got up, and the liquor started oozing out of his pores.

Mounting up, they rode down the silent street and into the desert.

⋆   ⋆   ⋆

On the other side of Desert Wells, a few hours later, Link Hauser was giving the Gatling gun a final check before they pulled out.

⋆   ⋆   ⋆

In Driscol's boarding house, Crowe woke with an uneasy feeling in his gut.

At first he thought it was the redeye, but he came to realize that it was something else.

With an effort, he pushed himself up into a sitting position and reached for the redeye, pulled the cork and took a long drink. He coughed the redeye clear of his lungs, then swung himself round so that he had his feet on the floor. Grabbing his pants, he pulled them on, then his shirt and boots, finally he got into his rig. By this time he was breathing hard, and sweating the redeye out of his body.

Once he was dressed he caught hold of the handles of the wheelchair, and dragged himself into it. Lassiter had made sure that nothing was in his way to the door. Crowe wheeled himself across the room, and reached for the handle. Outside, the corridor was empty. He cursed volubly. Driscol's kid came out to see what the ruckus was.

He came towards Crowe, and made the mistake of getting too close.

'What's the matter, you crazy old drunk?'

Crowe grabbed him, and hauled him up close. Driscol's kid nearly threw up when he smelled Crowe's breath.

'I'll tell you what the matter is, you little bastard.' He narrowed his eyes, and pulled the kid even closer. 'Death's comin' here, an' it ain't far off, an' you an' me are gonna do somethin' about that Grim Ol' Reaper. Got it?'

The kid shook his head, like it was on a stick. 'I got you.'

'Get yer scrawny ass in there, an' get my rifle, an' a couple of boxes of shells. You'll find them in the saddlebag under the bed, an' while yer scrabblin' about under the bed, bring that bottle of redeye.'

'Yessuh,' the kid said, his voice shaking.

Crowe swung the chair round until he was facing the door.

'C'mon' kid, get a move on,' he snarled.

Eventually, the kid came out holding the stuff Crowe had sent him for.

'Careful with that redeye,' Crowe

yelled at him as the bottle started to slip out of the kids hands.

Crowe leaned forward and stopped it falling to the floor.

'Now you've got to get me up them stairs. Yer ol' man still got that room he stores stuff he ain't gonna use agin?'

The kid nodded. 'What d'you want to go up there for?'

'I told you, Death's comin' to Desert Wells an' I want to see him come. Now git up there.'

The kid was too scared to do anything but what he was told. Crowe wheeled himself to the bottom of the stairs.

'Take my gear up to that front room, an' be quick about it. We ain't got all day. Give me a hand gettin' out of this dang blasted chair.'

The kid dropped the stuff.

'Be careful,' Crowe told him, handing him the redeye.

The kid put it on the floor, and helped Crowe to get out of the chair.

'OK. Now get that stuff up into that

room, an' hurry up.'

Driscol's kid picked up Crowe's stuff and struggled up the stairs with it.

Crowe took another pull at the redeye. He looked up, the kid was struggling, and was sweating heavily. Crowe could hear his laboured breathing.

'Hurry up,' Crowe shouted up the stairs.

The kid disappeared round the bend in the banister. Crowe heard him put the stuff down and go inside. He waited, then he heard the kid coming out of the room. He saw him at the top of the stairs.

When he got down, he pushed out his hand. 'Git hold of it.'

The kid got hold of Crowe's hand, and took his weight, and struggled as Crowe dragged himself up the darkened stairs one at a time.

When they got to the top, Crowe said, 'Now get my chair an' don't forget the redeye.'

Driscol's kid went down again.

Crowe watched him pull the chair up the stairs with the redeye on the seat.

At the top of the stairs, Crowe took the redeye, and helped himself to another drink. The kid collapsed panting and sweating at the top stairs.

Crowe grinned, and offered him the redeye. The kid looked at him like he was a mad man, and shook his head.

'You ain't as stupid as you look,' Crowe said with a grin. 'Now yer feelin' better, get me in my chair agin.'

The kid got hold of his hand, and took the weight.

'Go an' find Donaldson. He won't be at home. Most likely he'll be in the cathouse. You tell him to git over here. Death's on its way.'

'But,' the kid started to say.

'Sorry kid,' Crowe told him, and felt in his shirt pocket for a coin.

The kid's eyes lit up. 'Wow, a double eagle.'

He almost fell down the stairs.

Crowe rolled himself into the room, with his belongings on his knee. The room was like the rest of the house, dark, and smelling of the desert. It took him a while to steer between the stuff up there. When he got to the window, he took his rifle and smashed the boards off.

The strong sunlight almost blinded him, and he had to put his hands to his eyes until they got used to it.

The kid ran down the stairs, and out into the street.

Big Lily's cathouse was an adobe building round the corner on the left.

There weren't many whores there, and those that were there were pretty mangy and pretty scrawny.

Donaldson let it be on account of how he got to have a free one, and how he got to get the pick of the bunch. Most times he picked the Mandingo who was the least ugly, and the least diseased.

Big Lily was a fat black woman with a white eye patch over the empty eye socket. She didn't take too kindly to being woken by Driscol's kid when he came knocking at the door.

'Aw right,' she yelled, falling out of bed.

Grabbing the handrail she pulled herself to her feet. Straightaway the room started to spin. Lily lurched to the door. At first the handle wouldn't turn, because her palms were so sweaty.

When she got to the door that led to the street, she didn't see the kid at first, because he was standing on the bottom step.

'Death's comin' to Desert Wells,' the kid said.

Big Lily looked down at him. 'What are you yappin' about kid?'

'Death's comin' to Desert Wells,' the kid yelled at her.

Big Lily tried to bend down, but her head spun and she felt that she was going to fall on top of the kid.

She squinted and recognized him.

'Yer ol' man?' she said. 'He ain't here.'

'It's Sheriff Donaldson I want.'

'Him? Yeah, he's here. What's this all about?'

'Jim Crowe, he said Death was comin' to Desert Wells.'

'Jim Crowe,' Big Lily hollered. 'If Death's gonna come, it's gonna come for him. I'll tell the sheriff, but if yer ol' man whips you for wastin' the sheriff's time, it's yer own lookout.'

She slammed the door, and went to find Sheriff Donaldson.

'What's all the racket about?' Donaldson was still half asleep, and not in a good mood.

'Driscol's kid's at the door squawkin' about Death comin' to Desert Wells,' she said. 'Hogwash.'

'Said Lassiter's pard, Crowe, sent him.'

'That crazy ol' man, he's out of his mind with drink,' Donaldson said sourly. 'I'd better come an' see him.'

'You goin' like that?' Big Lily asked him. Donaldson swore and went into the room to get his pants. Driscol's kid was still at the door when they got there.

'Death's comin' to Desert Wells,' he

started as soon as the door was opened.

'Quit that, kid,' Donaldson said.

'It was Crowe that told me to tell you.'

'Where is Crowe?' Donaldson asked him.

'At Pa's place in the old storeroom where Pa keeps the furniture he has no use fer. Got all his guns up there with him. Think he's gone mad.'

'He bin at the redeye?' Donaldson asked him, buttoning up his flies.

'A full bottle of redeye. His breath smells like somethin' that's bin dead a while.'

'I'll get over there,' Donaldson said. 'An' how come you ain't in church?'

'An' how come yer here?' the kid said, looking at Big Lily.

The whore took a step forward to slap him but over-balanced and finished up in the dust. The kid ran.

Donaldson stepped over the whore, and followed the kid out to the boarding house.

'When he got there, there were a

couple of late church-goers staring up at Crowe.

'Get yerselves some guns,' Crowe was yelling down at them.

'Get back in there, you crazy ol' drunk,' Donaldson shouted back.

'You see that cloud with Death ridin' in its saddle?' Crowe pointed with his rifle.

Donaldson looked at the kid. 'Get up there and tell me if you can see anythin'.'

Driscol's kid ran into the boarding house and up the stairs into the storeroom.

Crowe was still sticking his head out of the window.

The kid shaded his eyes, and took a look.

'He's right. There's a real big cloud comin' this way.'

4

Hauser had fixed the Gatling on the back of a wagon, and was manning it himself. The renegade band swept out of the rocks yelling as they came. The riders stormed into the street, and began firing as they came. Hauser was at the rear of the charge firing the Gatling at the buildings, and those who had missed death the first time round.

As soon as the kid screamed, Donaldson high-tailed it for his office, and grabbed his spare six-gun from the drawer, along with a handful of shells. He got out onto the veranda, pushing lead into his gun. He managed to get off one round before a burst from the Gatling stitched a line of holes along his belly. He fell, screaming to his knees. One of Hauser's boys came back, and put a bullet in his head.

'That'll settle the noisy bastard,' he

yelled hysterically, as Donaldson was flung backwards, the last of his guts tipping out of his belly.

Crowe had levered some lead into the Winchester and got off a couple of rounds, bringing down one of Hauser's boys. Crowe's second piece of lead took a chunk of wood out of the side of a wagon. Hauser didn't notice it, as he kept on cranking the handle.

Those townsfolk that were in their houses ran into the street, those in the street, ran into the first shelter they could see. Hauser had the wagon turned at the end of the street, and started for a second run. This time he noticed Crowe's bullet as it hit his loader in the chest.

In surprise he looked up at where the piece of lead had come from. He swung the Gatling round, but he couldn't get the elevation. Crowe saw him and fired at him, grazing Hauser's shoulder. Hauser yelled.

'Get us out of here,' he shouted over his shoulder to the wagon driver.

The driver hauled into an alley.

'Get Ralston, an' a new loader,' Hauser told him when he had kicked the loader off the wagon.

'Right, boss,' the driver shouted over the firing that was going on.

Milt Ralston was Hauser's second in command. He was starting to herd the numbed townsfolk towards the church when the driver found him.

'Boss wants you,' he said to Ralston.

Ralston holstered his six-shooter, and got out of the saddle. He found Hauser crouched in the alley.

'What is it, boss?' he asked as another piece of lead from Crowe slammed into the wood by his head.

'That's what it is,' Hauser said, pointing with his six-gun towards the window.

Crowe leaned out of the window to see how things were going. Hauser just missed him.

'That fella' goin' to give us some trouble,' he said, his thick eyebrows meeting over his hawk nose as he frowned. 'I want you to get him down. I don't care how you do it, but make it quick.'

'Gotcha, Link,' Ralston said.

Bending double he ran from the alley.

Up in the storeroom, Crowe saw him making a break for it. He levered a round into the Winchester, and drew a bead on Ralston. The shot missed him, but not by much and Ralston threw himself through the flimsy wooden door of the mercantile.

He ran through to the back, kicking stuff out of the way as he went.

'Git you next time,' Crowe muttered, picking up the bottle of redeye, and taking a noisy swig from it.

He had a quick look round. The floor by his wheelchair was covered with spent shells from the Winchester. Crowe checked his ammunition for the six-gun that was nestling in the holster that he had hung on the side of the chair.

'Not a bad mornin's work, but yer

still gonna have to wait a while fer me,' he murmured to the Grim Reaper, taking another swig from the bottle.

Hauser's men had rounded up the folks from the town, and had herded them into the new church where the pastor was giving them some words of comfort. The fella who ran the bank was being frogmarched by one of Hauser's boys into the Desert Wells Bank.

One of them slammed him up against the door. It flew open. Cautiously, he looked inside, and saw a terrified Miss Rimmer trying to hide behind the counter.

'Get him in here,' Curly told one of those outside. Mister Fogarty found himself propelled through the door by somebody's boot.

Curly grabbed him by the shirt front. 'Git that safe opened, an' don't tell us there's nothin' in it. We know there's some gold dust.'

He pushed Fogarty towards the safe. Grabbing him by the collar of his shirt, he forced him to his knees.

'What you doin' here on a Sunday mornin'?' Curly asked the teller.

'Checking the books. We've an audit comin' up,' she said nervously.

'We're gonna save you the trouble.' Curly laughed, sweeping the ledgers off the desk.

He holstered his gun, and tore her blouse open. 'Git her in here,' he said pointing to Fogarty's office. Miss Rimmer started to scream as they carried her in there.

Ralston came running into the bank. 'Yer fun's gonna have to wait. We got a chore.'

'I'll be back,' Curly said, following Ralston outside.

He followed Ralston to the mercantile.

'We're gonna need some dynamite,' he said as they went inside. 'The boss has got some fella that needs bringin' down a peg or two.'

Ralston and Curly went through the place until they found a steel safe tucked away in the back.

Ralston cursed. 'We're gonna have to find the fella that owns this place, an' git him to open it.'

Both men went out again, and headed for the church.

'Who owns the mercantile?' Ralston asked after everybody had gone quiet when he had fired a shot into the ceiling.

Sam Small was shaking when he stepped forward.

Ralston caught him by the shirt front.

'Where are you takin' me?' Small asked.

'To do some mercantilin',' Ralston told him, kicking him towards the store.

'Git that safe open,' he said, as he stood over the quaking store owner.

Small's finger grappled with the combination. They slipped off it a couple of times, as he struggled to control himself.

'C'mon, hurry it up,' Ralston said, prodding him in the back of the head with his gun.

'I'm doin' my best,' Small told him, his voice shaking.

The last tumbler clicked into place and he pulled the door open.

'Git the dynamite,' Ralston told Curly.

Curly reached into the safe, and found the dynamite along with a coil of fuse.

He showed it to Ralston.

'Should be enough,' Ralston said. He clubbed Small across the head.

Outside, things had calmed down a mite, as most of the townsfolk had been rounded up or killed.

Crowe sat watching the street below him, swatting away the flies that had come to drink his sweat.

'Go an' feed on them fellas,' he said, pointing them to the two bodies that were stiffening in the sun. A couple of Hauser's men had made a break for the boarding house, but Crowe had put some lead in them. One of them lay twitching in the sun. Crowe finished him off.

'You git that dynamite?' Hauser asked Ralston.

'Sure boss,' Ralston said, showing it to him.

'Be careful with that stuff. I don't want it goin' up in my face,' Hauser snarled. 'You see that window up there?' he said, pointing to the window of the storeroom. 'Get up there, an' git that fella down here, so we can ask him why he's doin' all these bad things to us.'

'Gotcha boss,' Ralston said, fixing the fuse up to the dynamite. 'Ready, Curly?'

Curly nodded.

'We'll go across the street, an' into the alley. There's gotta be a back way in,' Ralston said.

Handing the dynamite to Hauser, he checked his gun, relieved Hauser of the dynamite, and nodded to Curly.

They ran out of the alley, covered by the fire of some of the renegades in there. They ran bent double, fire from Crowe's Winchester kicking up the dust as they ran.

Suddenly Curly screamed and went down, blood bubbling from his chest.

Hauser signalled another across with a wave of his gun.

The fella ran out into Crowe's line of fire. He went down, his chest burst open like a melon.

Crowe grinned macabrely as he levered another round into the breach. He picked the bottle of redeye up and took another swig, then wiped his mouth with the back of his hand.

Hauser looked at the other two in the alley, and pointed his .45 at them.

'Both of you git over there,' he ordered them.

Both men looked at each other, but Hauser put a piece of lead at their feet.

Ralston watched impatiently from the alley while they made up their minds.

Crowe found the makings and built himself a stogie, the Winchester resting on his knees. He blew the smoke out of the window. Hauser took a shot at it. Crowe grinned.

The two men had just about made

up their minds. Both cocked their guns, and ran for the alley across the street. Crowe had stuck the stogie into the corner of his mouth. He sent another piece of lead down, and knocked one of them over.

The second fella joined Ralston in the alley.

'Let's git up there,' Ralston said to him.

They ran down the alley to the gate at the far end. Ralston opened it, and they went into the untidy yard at the back.

Ralston took a look round. The back door was in the middle of the wall. He checked his gun, and motioned his amigo towards it. He nodded in that direction.

They cat-footed toward it. Ralston lifted the latch and they went into the narrow corridor that led to the stairs. Above them Crowe was finishing his last stogie. He blew out the smoke, and tossed the end into the street.

Ralston had reached the foot of the

stairs. He started up. The stair creaked as he put his weight on it. Crowe sent a couple of pieces of lead into the alley where Hauser and his men were hiding.

The two men climbed the stairs cautiously, their guns ready. Outside the storeroom Ralston put his finger to his lips, and put his gun away. Passing the dynamite to his amigo, he pulled a box of lucifers out of his pocket, took one out of the box and struck it. The flame flared. Taking the dynamite he lit the fuse and kicked the door open, and tossed it in.

Crowe turned and saw the bundle of dynamite sail into the room. He picked the redeye up, put it to his lips and emptied it. The last drop was going down his throat when the room exploded.

Hauser let out a howl of pleasure when the bloodied remains of Crowe were tossed into the street by the force of the explosion, along with half the room. Ralston had run down the stairs when he had tossed the dynamite in through the door. He stood leaning against the banister breathing hard.

Hauser had come out into the street with the fellas who had been in the alley with him. He waited until Ralston came out of the alley.

'Let's go an' git this saloon opened up.'

Ralston laughed. 'I've got some unfinished business down at the bank. an' I don't want to keep her waitin' any longer than I have to.'

'Me an' the rest of the boys'll be in that saloon over there,' Hauser said pointing to the Last Drop.

Hauser and his boys opened up the saloon. He dragged Herve out of the back room along with the soiled doves.

'Enjoy yourselves,' he said, pushing the soiled doves towards his men, who greeted them with a roar of approval.

He grabbed Herve, 'Serve out yer best stuff.'

'Right Mister Hauser,' Herve gabbled.

'Mister Hauser,' Hauser said with a

laugh. 'That sounds real good. I might adopt this boy.'

The renegades drank the Last Drop dry, they danced and whooped on the bar, shot the mirror to pieces, so that it looked like a giant spider's web. They filled the playing cards with bullet holes.

Daybreak found most of them still drunk, and hungover, the inhabitants of Desert Wells either dead or too frightened to step out of doors. Hauser sent a couple of his more sober boys to round the rest of his crew up, and get ready to leave.

He got them to fill up a wagon with food and a couple of barrels of water, and what they had taken from the bank. The ragged train pulled out of Desert Wells with a mess of outriders, and a second wagon carrying the Gatling gun.

★　★　★

A cold feeling came over Lassiter that morning shortly after he woke. As he fixed breakfast for them the cold certainty that Crowe was dead came over him. He looked back in the direction of Desert Wells. Yeah, Crowe was dead but it was something more than that. Something had happened in Desert Wells.

'What's bitin' him?' Trantor asked the woman as they walked towards the fire that Lassiter was building.

'Dunno,' was the answer.

'You folks sleep all right?' Lassiter asked them as he poured coffee into a couple of mugs.

'Fine,' Jennifer said, taking the coffee and putting it to her lips.

Trantor said nothing as he took his mug.

Over the ridge, Jim Fuller was watching everything that was going on. Fuller had risen an hour earlier, and breakfasted, before cleaning and loading his rifle. He figured that if he hit them now they would die out in the Cauldron.

Taking the Winchester from out of

the saddle-holster, which he had covered with a cloth to stop the sand fouling it up, he checked the chamber, and levered a round into the breach.

Lassiter had put the waterskins on the one side, and the bag holding the food on the other side of the packhorse. As Lassiter raised his own mug to his lips, Fuller drew a bead on the waterskins, and squeezed the trigger. The rifle bucked slightly as he fired. Below him, the bullet passed through the waterskin. Fuller fired again, straightaway, and the second waterskin burst, as the animal fell.

Lassiter dropped his mug, pulled out his .45, and looked in the direction of the ridge. Trantor hauled out his own gun, and pushed Jennifer out of the way.

'He's up there,' he said, pointing to the ridge.

Fuller saw them spreading out to take him from both sides. Levering a third round into the breech, he drew a bead on Trantor, and squeezed the trigger.

Trantor put his hand to his forehead, and staggered back, his knees buckling as he fell.

Jennifer ran towards him, her face white. Lassiter continued his run towards the ridge. Fuller grabbed the cloth at his side, got up, and ran for his horses.

As Lassiter reached the top of the ridge, he was in time to see Fuller galloping away. He watched the dust as it rose under the hoofs of Fuller's horses. He dropped the .45 back into the leather, and went back to where Trantor was lying.

The first thing he saw was Jennifer bent over Trantor, her shoulders shaking as she wept. He put his hand under her shoulder, and raised her so he could get a look at Trantor.

'He's dead,' Jennifer said, her voice shaking.

Lassiter glanced at Trantor's head. 'We'd better get him buried, before the vultures get at him.'

'What kind of a man are you?' she screamed at him, beating at his chest.

'He's only just bin shot, an' yer talkin' about buryin' him so the damn vultures don't get at him.'

Lassiter took a step back to regain his balance. He caught her wrists, and held them. 'Take it easy. This won't do you or him any good. Yer wastin' energy an' sweat in this heat.'

She steadied a mite, then fell forward into his arms. Lassiter picked her up, and carried her over to where her horse stood. He laid her on the sand, and put a saddle blanket over her. Behind him, the flies were collecting over Trantor's body. He shooed them away, but they only stayed away until Lassiter had gone to find a place to bury Trantor. When he found it, he started to scrape out a hole using his knife.

The job was a long one, and the sand kept sliding into the hole. Trantor's face had already gone black and was starting to swell. Putting his bandana over his mouth, he dragged Trantor over to the hole, and tipped him in. A few rocks lay close by.

Lassiter picked them up, and put them on the grave, figuring it was the best he could do to keep the scavengers from feeding off Trantor.

This done, he went to see if Jennifer was showing any signs of coming round. When he got over to her, he could see that some of the colour had come back to her face.

'Feelin' any better?' he asked her as she opened her eyes.

'He's dead, isn't he?' was the first thing she asked Lassiter.

'It was quick. I've known men stagger around in the desert for a couple of days, out of their heads because they had no water.'

It was when she started to sob, that he realized how tactless he had been.

Lassiter backed off until she got over it.

Finally, he got his canteen, and went back to her.

'Better have a swallow of this. You've bin out a spell, an' you're gonna need the water.'

She took the canteen, and had a swallow from it.

'I buried him over here,' Lassiter said to her. 'There's some wild flowers if you want somethin' to put on his grave. Can't seem to find anythin' to make a marker with, though.'

She pushed herself up into a sitting position and looked to where Lassiter had buried Trantor. 'It doesn't matter. One place is as good as another.'

Lassiter helped her up. 'Come on down there an' you can pick yer flowers,' he said.

When he got her to her feet, he found that she was shaking. For a while they stood over the grave. Lassiter was wondering if he should offer to say something, but then he didn't know the fella, and there was something about them both that didn't set right.

In the end it was the girl who broke the silence. 'We'd better be gettin' on before it gets too hot.'

Lassiter watched her. 'Ain't that simple. That fella not only shot the horse, he blew a couple of holes in the waterskins. All we've got is what we got in our canteens.'

For the first time he saw fear in her face. 'You mean we ain't got enough water to get to Spanish Wells?'

'I didn't say that. It's gonna be hard, but I know where there is some water. It's an old waterhole the Indians use. Ned Butler showed it to me. Good thing he did before your friend shot him.'

Her face coloured up. 'Jim Fuller ain't no friend of mine.' She stopped short, realizing she might have said too much.

Lassiter grabbed her by the arms. 'Just who is this Jim Fuller? Why did he kill Ned? Ned never cheated at anythin' includin' cards, in his life,' he shook her angrily.

'Jim Fuller shot my husband. He reckoned my husband stole some money off him,' she lied.

'Then what's he doin' out here?' Lassiter demanded.

'He reckons my husband told me where the money is.'

Lassiter let her go. He didn't know whether she was telling him the truth or not. 'Make sure your canteen's OK then get mounted an' we'll go an' git some water.'

He examined the two waterskins. There wasn't any point in trying to do anything with either of them. They wouldn't be holding any more water. He shook his own canteen, and got into the saddle.

'Just follow me,' Lassiter said.

He gigged his horse in the direction from which Fuller's firing had come. At the top of the ridge, he hauled on the leathers, and looked across the sands to get his bearings.

Lassiter gigged the horse, and they rode down the slope.

'God, I hate this desert,' Jennifer said after a while.

She sounded tired, and angry. Lassiter said nothing. He hadn't believed much of what she had said. He watched as she reached for the canteen.

'Leave it,' he told her. 'That water's got to last you.'

She stopped and put the canteen back on the saddle-horn.

'How long is it before we get there?' she asked peevishly.

'All today, and some of tomorrow,' he replied without turning in her direction.

'Almost two days,' she groaned.

'Save it,' Lassiter said. 'Yer gonna need it.'

She went quiet.

5

Ralph Gillespie and Jake Galloway hauled up at the edge of Desert Wells.

'Musta bin the hell of a storm,' Gillespie said, biting off a hunk of chewing tobacco.

He handed it across to Jake Galloway, who waved it away.

'That's a filthy habit,' he said, as he surveyed the damage that Hauser and his boys had done.

A lot of the buildings had been damaged, and a pile of bodies was building up a few feet away.

'Startin' to whiff a mite,' Gillespie said, wiping the tobacco juice off his mouth with the back of his hand. 'Guess the best place to start is the sheriff's office.'

Galloway laughed at this. 'It's over there.'

They gigged their horses over in the direction of Donaldson's office, and slid out of their saddles when they got there. Galloway hitched the horses to the rail, while Gillespie gave the town the once over. There weren't many people about and those that were looked like they still couldn't believe what had happened.

Gillespie knocked on the door, and went in to an empty office.

'Anybody around?' he called out while Galloway went over to the dodger posters lying on the cabinet.

When he got no answer Gillespie called out again.

'Say, take a gander at these.' Galloway laughed.

His amigo went over to where he was standing, and took the posters that he was holding.

'It's more like yer horse than you,' Gillespie said, making the spittoon rattle as he sent his chaw of tobacco rattling into it.

Both men stopped what they were doing and looked in the direction of the door leading to the cells.

'What do you reckon that was?' Galloway asked, heading for the door.

'Best way to find out is to take a look,' Gillespie said, easing up the latch and going into the short corridor.

They walked along to the bottom cell. They saw a pale figure crouching on his bunk. The fella struggled off the bunk, and hobbled towards them.

'Water,' he croaked. 'For pity's sake, water.'

The two men looked at each other. Gillespie nodded in the direction of the door.

'He'll get you some water. While we're waitin' fer him to get back, just tell me what happened here, pardner.'

'Git me the water. I can't hold out much longer,' the fella croaked, hanging onto the bars.

Galloway came back with his canteen, and took the stopper off. Gillespie took it off him, and held it just out of reach of the prisoner.

'Give me some water,' the prisoner pleaded.

'When you tell us what happened here,' Gillespie said, tipping the canteen so that some of the water spilled out onto the floor.

A pair of fevered eyes in the cell widened in fear and hate.

'All right, I'll tell you,' he gasped. 'We got hit by Link Hauser. He had a Gatling with him.'

'Any idea where he's headed?'

'Went off in the direction of Spanish Wells. Now, the water for God's sake.'

Gillespie pushed the canteen through the bars, and let the fella drink from it, then pulled it back away from the grasping hands.

Galloway and Gillespie looked at each other.

'What are you in here for?'

'Drunk and disorderly,' was the reply.

Galloway laughed. 'Where's the sheriff?'

'On Boot Hill with a lot of other people. Heard Herve, the barkeep down at the Last Drop, tellin' Driscol.' The fella wiped his mouth with the back of his hand. 'Got any more water in that canteen?'

Gillespie rattled the canteen. 'Some.'

The fella in the cell gave him a supplicating look.

Gillespie looked at Galloway.

'He ain't done us any harm,' Galloway said.

'Naw, he ain't at that,' Gillespie said, pushing the canteen through the bars where a pair of greedy hands snatched it from him.

'You fellas have bin real good to me. How about tellin' somebody I'm in here so I can get back to my wife. She'll be worried sick about me.'

Gillespie laughed. 'Yer a dangerous fella. The town's better off with you where you are.'

Galloway was about to say something else when Gillespie jerked his head in the direction of the office. They left the fella in the cell emptying the canteen.

'You reckon Hauser's got word of where the gold is?' Galloway asked his amigo when they were in the office.

Gillespie thought about it. 'Might have. He's got himself a Gatling, so he might be on his way to get it.'

'Never figured on Hauser gettin' to know about it or goin' up to Spanish Wells. An' that Gatling's gonna make things even harder.'

'We'd best be gettin' some supplies an' another horse to carry them.' Gillespie said.

The street had emptied like a second shock wave had hit the town.

Nobody was in the mercantile. Taking a couple of gunnysacks, they filled them with stuff from the shelves.

'All we need now is a horse, an' some water,' Gillespie said.

It didn't take too long to get that stuff together.

As they rode out, Galloway looked over his shoulder, and thought he was looking at a ghost town.

6

Fuller had slowed the horses to a walk once he got clear of the place where he had shot Trantor.

He watched as the sun rose in the sky, and figured that Jennifer and the fella who was taking her across the Cauldron would have to take it slow as well. He regretted that he hadn't shot the other horses, but Trantor and the other fella had been so damn quick. He barely had time to get to his horse before they got to the top of the ridge.

Slowing his horse he gigged her into the shadow of a mess of rocks, and got down. Fuller took off his hat and wiped the sweat from the brim and then his forehead. After he had fed the horses and watered them, he got himself a drink, and cut himself a piece of dried meat. It was real hot, and he lazed back against a rock, his hat pulled down over his eyes. He figured he was safe for a spell. His eyes drooped shut, and he fell into a light doze, until the prodding of a rifle barrel in his belly roused him.

Fuller tried to jump to his feet, but the pressure of the rifle pushed him back to the ground.

'Jus' keep yer ornery self nice an' still, an' you won't get a bullet.' The voice was old and croaky, and sounded like it had been in the desert for a long time.

Fuller opened his eyes, and squinted against the sun.

The rifle was pressed firmly into his belly. The voice croaked on. 'I'm jus' gonna relieve you of that fancy shootin' iron, so don't do anythin' stupid. My eyesight ain't what it was, but I don't reckon I can miss from here.'

The old fella reached forward, and took Fuller's gun out of the leather. He broke open the chamber, and let the cartridges fall into the sand.

'Now git up, an' collect them horses,' the old man said, prodding Fuller in the back with the rifle.

Fuller walked over to the horses, and caught hold of the leathers.

'That way, through that openin' in the rocks,' he was told.

Fuller led the horses from the sunlight into the darkness of the opening.

Above him he could still see the sky. The gully took a downward course.

'Yer doin' fine,' he heard the old man behind him. 'Go to yer right here, an' stop.'

Fuller stopped in front of a small cabin, with two mules tethered outside.

He felt his hands being grabbed from behind, and fastened with a rope.

From the corner of his eye, he saw the old man tethering the horses to a hitch rail where the mules were hitched.

He was prodded in the back again with the rifle. The old man prodded him through a break in the rocks, and he came into a cave.

'This is Martha, my wife, an' I'm Mike. Go across an' say hello to Martha.'

Fuller's eyes had got used to the

gloom in the cave. With a prod from Mike's gun, he stumbled across to his wife. When he got there, he froze. The woman was dead. Fuller could see that she hadn't been dead too long.

'Hi,' he heard himself say.

'Martha ain't feelin' too talkative since her old beau, Sid, died on her, in't that so, Martha?' Mike asked, his voice rising as he spoke.

'I'm gonna give you an easy start,' Mike said. 'I need some help in this mine since Sid ran out on me. Near broke Martha's heart, didn't it?' he babbled on.

'What d'you mean?' Fuller asked him.

The old man laughed. 'There's a heap of gold in here, only it ain't gonna come crawlin' out. Me an' you, we're gonna have to go in an' get it.'

Fuller hadn't reckoned on this. He had gold waiting for him, and he didn't intend to go digging for it. Whelan was going to tell him where it was, whether he wanted to or not.

'While yer new to the family, you can get off to an easy start. Take a day off so you can get yer strength fer the mornin',' Mike cackled.

He filled out two mugs with water, and unfastened Fuller's hands so he could drink it.

Mike sat silently on a crate, the rifle across his knees.

'Aw right, that's enough,' he told Fuller. 'Git on yer feet,'

He prodded Fuller out of the cave and down a narrow tunnel, lit by candles pushed into the cracks in the walls. He prodded him into a cave like the one they'd just left. There was a bunk in the corner with two iron rings driven into the rock.

'Turn round,' Mike said.

As Fuller turned, Mike hit him with the butt of the rifle.

Mike went back to where Martha was sitting on the crate. He poured himself a shot of redeye into a mug.

'Good to have some company agin, ain't it?' he said to her. 'Shame about

Sid. Shoulda kept his hands to himself, an' not gone tryin' to paw you every time my back was turned. Once that young fella's had a good night's sleep he'll be ready to empty this mine of gold.'

Fuller soon gave up struggling against the chains. There was no give in them, and he figured he would need his strength to figure a way out of this rattrap.

Fuller calmed himself, and finally got off to sleep. In the first cave that the crazy miner had taken him to, Mike had carried Martha to the double bunk, and had settled down beside her.

★   ★   ★

Lassiter had found some shelter for him and Jennifer.

They had bedded down in the shelter of some rocks, and he had built a fire. Lassiter had taken some of the provisions from one of the gunny-sacks he had taken from the back of the packhorse. While Jennifer sat in silence, he fixed up a meal for them. At first, she had picked at the grub, but her appetite had come back to her, and she ate hungrily.

Lassiter ate slowly, his mind on the well near the ruined town of Kaiserberg. If the well was still giving water, and nothing happened to the horses, he reckoned they would have enough to get to Spanish Wells.

When he had finished eating, he took the cap off a canteen and handed it to Jennifer. She gave him a smile, and took the canteen.

To his surprise she moved up closer to him.

'You know,' she said. 'I like to know something about the people I'm travelling with. Tell me about yerself.'

Suddenly Lassiter was flattered by her attention. He shrugged.

'Nothin' to tell.'

'Ned Butler showed you this well, didn't he?'

'Yeah, me an' Crowe, that's my

partner,' he stopped speaking. 'He was my partner; I think he's dead now. We come up here a few years back huntin' fer some fella that'd pulled a couple of robberies near Spanish Wells. This fella took some catchin', an' Ned showed us all over the Cauldron while we were at it.'

He felt her stiffen beside him.

'You were lawmen?' she asked.

'In a manner of speakin'. Me an' Crowe wuz bounty hunters,' he said, feeling her ease away from him a mite.

'How come you know yer partner's dead?' she asked.

'Ain't rightly sure, just a feelin' I got. When you go bounty huntin' with a fella, you get to sense things about him, an' I sensed he was dead.'

She didn't say anything.

Lassiter stifled a yawn. 'Time to be turnin' in,' he said.

Jennifer pulled away from him; and got down in her blanket, glad that Lassiter had not been able to see her face. It had come as the hell of a shock when he told her that he was a bounty hunter. She wondered why he had not recognized her name. Pulling a robbery that size had shaken everybody up.

The following morning, they moved towards the Indian waterhole. She watched Lassiter out of the corner of her eye, wondering if he had made the connection.

★ ★ ★

Fuller was woken up by Mike shaking his shoulder. The old man had a grip like a vulture. His bony finger dug deep into Fuller's flesh, causing him to wake with a start.

'Glad to see yer awake,' the old fella cackled. He took the key, and put it in the lock. He twisted it, and Fuller felt the lock open.

'Jus' follow me, an' there ain't no point tryin' anythin' fancy. You just wouldn't git outta here.'

Fuller trailed after him to where

Martha sat, a plate of food in front of her.

'Sit yerself here,' the miner said, pointing to a crate opposite Martha.

A cold shiver ran through him as he stared at the cadaver across from him.

'Thought of all that hard work makin' you go cold?' Mike said with a sarcastic relish.

Fuller said nothing as Mike served up some ham and eggs that he had cooked over an open fire in the cave. He poured three mugs of coffee, and put one in front of Martha.

'Feelin' off yer food, Martha darlin'?' the miner asked her. 'Get like that sometimes. Sometimes she goes all day without eatin' or drinkin',' he said conversationally to Fuller.

Fuller watched the miner's face. When he had woken that morning, he had hoped the whole thing had been some sort of hellish dream. Knowing what was ahead of him, and that he would need all his strength to get through the day, and figure a way of getting out of the madman's clutches, he started to cut up his ham. At least he wouldn't have Martha to worry about. He gave a macabre smile.

'Glad to see something's tickled you,' he heard the miner say.

When Mike had finished eating, he got up. 'Time to get to work.'

He shackled Fuller's feet together before they got out into the mine. Mike put the key into his vest pocket. He gave Fuller a pick when they got into the mine.

Fuller wasn't that bothered about the mining, his two years in the prison quarry breaking rock had built him up. Mike followed him along the dark passageway until they reached the face.

'This is where we start,' he said, dropping his pick at his feet. Fuller noticed that he had discarded the rifle, and a pistol was stuck in his belt.

Fuller swung at the rock face. Mike was nearby, but out of his reach. There was no hope of swinging the pick at him. Both men worked steadily for an hour, hacking the rock from the face. After an hour Mike wiped the sweat from his face, and picked up the canteen that he had brought with him. Taking the cap out, he put it to his lips and took a long swallow. Fuller watched as the water ran down Mike's lips, and through the dust that had settled there.

He wiped his own mouth.

'I could use a swallow of that.'

Mike took the canteen from his mouth. 'Guess you could at that.'

He replaced the cap, and tossed the canteen to Fuller.

Fuller caught it, and took a drink. Mike had turned his back and bent down to examine the rock at his feet. Fuller braced himself, took a step forward. Mike heard him, but it was too late. Fuller crashed the canteen down on his head again and again.

The miner lay still at his feet. Fuller threw the canteen away, and turned Mike over to get his key out of his pocket. He took the key and unfastened the shackles. Viciously, he kicked the dead man in the ribs, and went back to where Martha was sat up on the crate, looking at her breakfast.

He leaned over, and took the plate from in front of her. ''Scuse me, pretty lady,' he said with a laugh.

Fuller ate quickly. The hours hacking at the rock face and beating the miner with the canteen had given him an appetite.

Tossing the plate in the corner, he searched round until he had found his gun and holster. Being a careful man with his tools he fastened on his holster, and checked the gun. When he had dropped it in the leather, he took a quick look round the cave, tipped his hat to Martha and went to find his horses.

The horses were still tethered outside. Fuller guessed that Mike hadn't had time to unload them, so greedy was he to get to the gold. Checking them over, Fuller climbed into the saddle, and headed towards Spanish Wells.

7

Lassiter and Jennifer had got an early start before the sun could get up high enough to do them any damage, but it was still damned hot, and the desert shimmered before them. The high rocks seemed to sway from side to side, and Lassiter couldn't stop the sweat running down his face, and through his stubble. He scratched at it until it was red and in some places bleeding. His bandanna stuck to the back of his neck like a rubbery second skin. A few feet away, he could see that the girl was faring even worse. He leaned over and caught the bridle of her horse, as she was about to fall out of the saddle.

She jerked herself upright, and gave him a sleepy grin.

'We're gonna have to stop a spell. It's even hotter than yesterday.'

Jennifer nodded her head weakly, and

Lassiter thought she was going to pass out. He eased her out of the saddle, took the blanket from behind her horse and laid it over her to keep the sun off her.

Guiding her horse, he got it to its knees so that it could give her some more shade. From his own horse he took his canteen, and wiped her lips with the water he had put on his fingers. Her eyes flickered open. Lassiter rubbed some more water on to her lips.

'Drink some of this. Just a mouthful,' he said.

Jennifer nodded weakly, and Lassiter put the canteen to her cracked lips.

As she took the water, she tried to grab the canteen.

'Sorry,' Lassiter told her. 'That's enough for now.'

As he turned away, she caught hold of his arm.

'What is it?' he asked her.

'I'm sorry about Ned Butler. Jim Fuller killed him. Fuller's a cold-blooded fella. He shouldn't have done it.'

'Who's Jim Fuller?' Lassiter asked her, afraid that she would pass out before she could tell him.

'He's the fella that got us in this mess,' she said, her voice thick with the lack of water.

'Why'd he kill Ned?' Lassiter asked her.

'Because Butler was gonna get us across the Cauldron,' she said.

Lassiter fed her some more water. 'I don't follow. You wanted Ned to get you across the Cauldron so you could see yer husband before he died,' Lassiter said in a puzzled voice.

'My husband won't be dying until I put a bullet in him,' she said starkly.

'Why'd you want to kill yer husband?'

'I thought you'd have figured that out last night when you told me you were a bounty hunter. You an' Crowe, I think you said his name was.'

'Crowe, that was his name,' Lassiter told her. 'But why should I figure it out?'

'You an' Crowe are bounty hunters. Five years back my husband, Fuller, Trantor an' three other fellas stuck up a train in these parts stuffed with gold. They got clean away.'

Lassiter thought about it. 'I remember hearin' about it. Me an' Crowe was up north tryin' to get some woman an' her kid up to Loganberry. Heard about it when we got back here. Never got any names though.'

'Everythin' went fine,' she said, after Lassiter had given her some more water. 'Real fine, except that Jack, my husband, got greedy. He took off with the gold. Sold everybody out to the law. They did their time, an' now they're out lookin' fer the gold and Jack.'

'I remember Donaldson tellin' me about it,' Lassiter said thoughtfully.

He looked down at Jennifer, but she had passed out.

Standing up, Lassiter put the canteen to his lips and took a drink. Jim Fuller and Spanish Wells. He was going to get up there, find Fuller, and put him down for what he did to Ned. As he thought about it, he realized that if he got the gold back, there would be a reward in it. He had another drink, swirled it round in his mouth and spat it out. Suddenly he felt a heap better. He'd drink to Crowe and Ned until he dropped, then buy them the best headstones that money could run to. Yeah, things were looking up. He wiped his face with his hand. The Cauldron was living up to its name. He took the makings out of his vest pocket, and built himself a stogie.

Overhead, the sun grew hotter, and the day brighter, then the sun began to fall below the horizon, and the temperature with it. Lassiter let Jennifer wake up in her own time.

When she did wake up, he offered her a mug of water. She sat up, her back against her saddle.

'How long was I out?' she asked him when she had drunk some of the water.

'Most of the day,' Lassiter said, watching her face. 'We'd best be gettin'' on pretty soon, I want to be there before mornin' or we just ain't gonna have enough water to see us through.'

She got up with Lassiter's help, and stood for a moment, swaying on her feet.

'You all right?'

'Yeah, I'm fine. I must have still bin a mite woozy.'

He saddled her horse for her, then helped her up into the saddle.

They moved out in the direction of Kaiserberg under a growing sky of stars.

For most of the night, they went on, until the sun started to come up, with a pink brush on the horizon.

'How's it goin'?' Lassiter asked her.

'Bin better, bin worse,' she said with a lopsided grin.

'We're nearly there,' Lassiter replied.

'Glad to hear it,' was the reply.

The ruins of Kaiserberg came into sight gradually. It was a sawtooth of broken-down houses that had been no better than shacks. Lassiter led her through what had been the main street of the town.

'What happened here?' she asked him.

'The desert and the weather happened here,' Lassiter told her, looking round. 'Just came creeping in. Nothing nor nobody could stop it. Just kept on creepin' in.'

Jennifer looked at him, but said nothing.

'The water's just outside of town. A clump of rocks, and it's just behind there,' Lassiter said, reaching onto his pommel for the canteen.

He put it to his mouth. Empty. He watched Jennifer take a drink from her canteen. She was about to drop the canteen into the sand.

'You'd better hold on to it. There's water out there, but no canteens to put it in.'

She hung it on the pommel again, and followed him.

It was half an hour later when they got to the waterhole.

'This is it,' Lassiter told her.

He helped her down, and took the rope from her saddle horn.

'What are you goin' to do with that?' she asked him.

'Give me them other canteens, an' I'll show you.'

She handed him the canteens and watched as he put them over his shoulder. Taking the rope, he dropped it round his waist, and tied the free end to the pommel of his horse. 'Hold this while I go over the edge,' he said, pointing to the lip of the waterhole. 'The water only comes down a drop at a time. Don't let anythin' spook the horses.'

At the edge of the waterhole, he turned his back on it, and inched his way down. For the first time in a while, he felt coolness coming from somewhere. A shiver ran through his body. Lassiter splayed out his legs, to support himself, and continued to inch his way down, his hands bracing himself against the sides of the hole, the canteens banging against his side as he went further down.

Above him, he could see the hole he had come through getting smaller, until his feet jarred on the rock that told him he had reached the bottom. Balancing himself, he took the stopper out of one of the canteens and held it under the drip of water. After a while, his arms started to ache with the strain. It seemed to take forever to get one of the canteens filled.

Lassiter replaced the top and slung the canteen over his shoulder. He rested his weight against the side of the hole, and relaxed. The relief from the cooling breeze had long since given way to a raging thirst in his mouth, and a burning ache in his joints. He took a drink from his own canteen, and rested his back against the side of the waterhole. After a while, he started to fill the second canteen. That seemed to take forever, but when it was done, he replaced the stopper, and hauled on the rope.

After a minute or so, the slack was

taken up, and he began to rise out of the waterhole. Slowly, the sun came over the rim.

'Glad to see you're with us again,' Jennifer said, helping him over the side of the hole. Her quick fingers soon got the rope unfastened, and over his body.

Quickly, Lassiter handed her one of the canteens, which she soon started to drink from.

'Go easy on that,' Lassiter said with a laugh. 'I've got to get over that rim again, an' fill up that other canteen.'

Jennifer gave a laugh, and handed the canteen to Lassiter.

'I've had an idea,' she said, showing him another rope. 'I got this off my pommel. Take this with you, an' tie the other canteen to it, an' send it up. I'll send this to you, so you can fill it up agin.'

Lassiter liked the idea. 'OK,' he said with a grin.

They basked in the sunshine for a spell, feeling a heap better now they had water.

'Should be in Spanish Wells late tomorrow,' Lassiter said.

'An' when you get to Spanish Wells, are you goin' lookin' for Fuller?'

'The minute we get there,' he said.

'And what about the gold?' she asked him.

Lassiter decided to lie. 'Gold ain't my concern. Gettin' even for Ned is though.'

The answer seemed to satisfy her.

'Let's get to work,' he said, taking another drink from the canteen, and pushing himself to his feet.

Holding the leathers of the horses, Jennifer lowered Lassiter into the hole again. Again, he started to fill the canteens.

'Hi, fella, you busy down there?'

The voice was totally unexpected. Lassiter almost dropped the canteen he was filling. Above him he saw the silhouette of a head.

'What's goin' on?' he shouted.

'We just came to relieve you of your horses an' yer woman.'

Lassiter heard Jennifer scream.

'Let her go, you bastard,' Lassiter shouted again, dangling on the rope.

'Or you'll do what, fella?' the voice came back. 'We'd like to stick around chewin' the fat, but the boss wants to see us before we get to Spanish Wells.'

The end of the rope fastened to the horses came hurtling towards Lassiter.

Losing his balance, Lassiter fell against the side of the waterhole. His head hit the rock with a crack, and he blacked out.

The bounty hunter came round to find himself lying on the rock at the bottom of the waterhole, with a steady drip of water hitting him in the face.

Pressing his hands against the side of the water-hole he got himself to his feet.

Above him, he could see the blue cloudless sky over his head. The sides of the waterhole were close enough for him to press against them with his hands, and do the same with his feet. Taking a last look up, he saw the sky, and started to prise himself out of the waterhole moving crabwise.

It didn't take long before cramp set in, and Lassiter tried to ease his body as he went up. He felt like he had been in the waterhole since forever when he finally grabbed the lip, and hauled himself out. For a while he lay there, letting the aching leave his body.

Getting up, Lassiter could see that there was nothing left; along with Jennifer, they had taken the horses. He had his six-gun, which was still dry, and one canteen of water.

Up in the sky, he could see that there would be no let up in the heat. He looked at the tracks left by the man who had taken Jennifer. They were pointing further into the desert. Reluctant that he could do nothing for Jennifer straight off, he started walking in the direction of Spanish Wells.

8

Jennifer hadn't seen the three men coming her way, she had been busy peering into the water-hole to see how Lassiter was doing.

The first thing she knew about anything being wrong was when a rope looped over her waist, and she was dragged away from the waterhole.

'Caught ourselves a she-devil,' the fella holding the rope sang out, as he pulled her towards him.

Jennifer caught hold of the rope and tried to pull at the horse, but the stranger gigged the horse backwards, and she sprawled in the dust.

Wrapping the end of the rope round his pommel, he jumped out of the saddle, along with the other two. He took the rope off her, and grabbed her round the waist before she could squirm away.

He fastened his mouth on hers, but Jennifer brought her knee up into his groin. He let out a yell that turned into a laugh, as one of his *compadres* caught her and tried the same thing. Jennifer braced herself, but it wasn't going to work a second time.

The second man caught her knee as it came up, and a hefty push sent her to the ground. His amigo grabbed her, and pinned her to the ground.

'Lefty, we ain't here fer that,' the first man said, massaging his groin.

'Shame,' Lefty said, as he turned round, seeming to see the horses for the first time. 'Seems like she ain't here by herself. Gonna take a look, Harry?'

Fielding moved over to the edge of the well, and looked into it.

'There's somebody in there, all right,' he said to the others, taking his knife out of the sheath at his back.

Fielding and Lassiter exchanged words.

'Just cut it,' Lance Dexter shouted to him.

Fielding cut the rope. Dexter caught Jennifer, and hauled her to her feet.

'What's a pretty thing like you doin' out here all alone?' he asked her.

'I ain't all alone,' she said.

'You are now,' Bill Harmon said.

Fielding came over to join them. 'Let's try agin, or you ain't gonna be so pretty,' he said, drawing his knife, and running the sharp edge along Jennifer's cheek.

She knew he meant what he said. A man like this was on his way to Spanish Wells to do the same thing to her husband, if she didn't get there before him.

'I was on my way to Spanish Wells to see my husband, but the cavalry wouldn't let us go any further because of Link Hauser.'

The three men laughed at this. 'You'd have bin safer in Desert Wells,' Dexter said.

'While we're riding in that direction we'll take you that way. Won't we, boys?'

'An' Link might like to talk to her,' Fielding said. 'Now get on that horse, an' we'll go see Link, an' the rest of the boys. We'll take them horses with us. They ain't gonna be any use to whoever's in that hole.'

Dexter pushed Jennifer up into the saddle. He took hold of the leathers and they headed out to where Hauser was camped.

The first thing that she saw was Hauser holding a cloth as he cleaned the dust off the Gatling.

'We found this over near that set of wrecked buildings,' Dexter said when Hauser got off the wagon.

He dragged her out of the saddle and dumped her at Hauser's feet.

Hauser turned her over with his foot, and examined her like a rancher examining a prize longhorn.

'Fair lookin' piece of stuff,' he said. 'You've done right well. They'll pay a good price for her over the border.'

Jennifer shuddered when she heard this.

'For now take her and put her in the wagon, an' make sure nobody damages the goods,' Hauser said.

Dexter caught her under the arm, and pushed her towards the wagon behind the one the Gatling was on.

'Just get in there,' he said, pushing her up into the wagon.

The inside of the wagon was hot, and stuffy. Jennifer flopped onto a couple of empty sacks, and closed her eyes.

If the renegades hadn't shown up, she would have been on her way to Spanish Wells, with Lassiter still in the well and trying to work out how to get out of it. Instead, she was stuck in the back of the wagon being held prisoner by a bunch of no-good cutthroats. She was going to Spanish Wells, sure, but having seen the Gatling she wondered what Hauser had in mind for the town. She lay on her back watching the canvas of the wagon starting to move as the wind got up. She tried to work out why Hauser would want to go to Spanish Wells. There wasn't anything there. The wind blew away part of the canvas top. The sun shone directly into her eyes, like a golden light, she thought. Yes, that was it. Somehow Hauser had got word that Whelan had stashed the gold up there somewhere, and was going after it.

★ ★ ★

Lassiter was heading off in the same direction. There wasn't much he could do about Jennifer, and, besides, he had to meet with Fuller in Spanish Wells. He wondered if the ex-Ranger Bill Faber was hanging about round there. Bill had collected a bullet in the leg a while back and had to quit the Rangers. He knew Spanish Wells intimately. If Fuller was in Spanish Wells, Bill Faber would get to know about it. Lassiter resisted the temptation to take a drink, as he tramped on through the day.

★ ★ ★

Galloway and Gillespie were heading up to Spanish Wells at a pretty fair rate, and not sparing the horses with Fuller up ahead of them, as anxious to get his hands on the gold as they were.

Fuller had got to Spanish Wells by riding one of the miner's horses until it dropped. He had then switched to his own, and taken it a mite easier. He reached the outskirts of the town at the same time Jennifer had decided to do a deal with Hauser.

Spanish Wells was a bigger place than Desert Wells, and had a few more people than Desert Wells. He gigged his horse down the main street looking for somewhere to stay until he could find Whelan, and ask him where the gold was.

He found one at the end of the street. A small adobe building that put him in mind of Driscol's place. Hitching his horse to the rail, he went inside. A thin Mexican woman lazed behind the counter. She looked up in an unfriendly way when he came towards her.

'I want a room for a couple of nights,' he told her.

'It will cost you, *señor*,' she said.

'I didn't expect to get it free,' Fuller said, as he dropped his saddlebag on the floor.

The woman concealed her contempt for the dangerous gringo. 'There ees a room at the back. I weel show it to you.'

'How much?' Fuller asked her.

'Ten pesos a night, *señor*.'

'Ten pesos?' Fuller demanded angrily.

'If you pay five pesos we will be obliged to inform the authorities that there is a stranger in town. Link Hauser, the renegade, is making trouble for the Yankees,' she said.

Fuller knew that he had no choice but to pay what she asked, and he thought maybe he could use her to get a line on Whelan. 'That'll be just fine,' he said, taking out his billfold.

She watched as he peeled off the pesos.

The woman waited while he picked up his saddlebag. She led him along a corridor to the room, which was small and untidy.

'If there is any need for you to get out of this room queeckly,' she said, 'the window leads to the garden, and out to the back of town.'

'*Gracias*,' Fuller told her.

She left him to get unpacked.

Fuller tossed his meagre belongings on the bed, and shook the pitcher on the small table, then poured some of the water in the bowl, and rinsed his face. Next he cleaned and checked his gun.

★　★　★

Lassiter was beginning to find the going real hard. He had held off taking a drink from the canteen, wanting to be able to hold out until nightfall, but his thirst finally got the better of him and he took the cork out and had a long drink.

His skin felt like scorching leather, his feet burned and he felt the shirt on his back was starting to scorch. Spanish Wells seemed to be further away than he remembered. He stumbled on with it getting harder and harder to put one foot in front of the other. In the end he went head down in the sand and couldn't force himself to his feet. It all went black. Then he was back at the water-hole, the drop of water falling onto his face, but it wasn't a drop. It was a whole torrent, and it was forcing itself into his mouth. He started panicking at the thought of drowning. The water was flooding into his mouth threatening to drown him. Lassiter started to struggle, but something was preventing him, stopping him from getting back into the light.

'Take it easy, Rafe,' the voice said.

Lassiter opened his eyes. This was the face of Death. Smiling, bearded, American with a Texas accent.

Lassiter started to struggle again to get to his feet, but the Texan angel held him down.

'Take it easy, Rafe. You're better off

where you are fer the time being.'

The angel knew his name.

'Come on Rafe, just hold still, I'll soon have you on yer feet again. It's me, Bill Faber.'

Lassiter's eyes snapped open again. Bill Faber. Yes, by God, it was Bill, and he wasn't dying, and he could still get Fuller. He relaxed.

'Glad to see you, Bill,' Lassiter said when he could speak.

'A surprise to see you,' Faber said with a crooked grin. 'A mite out of the way fer you, out here.'

'Could say the same for you,' Lassiter told him.

'What yer tryin' to say is, what am I doin' out here?'

'Yer a perceptive fella,' Lassiter said. 'What are you doin' out here?'

'Stranks came through Spanish Wells a couple of days ago, brought some interestin' news.'

'Let me tell you,' Lassiter interrupted him. 'Link Hauser's on the move. Got himself a Gatling from somewhere, an' the Mexcan Government is lettin' Stranks run him down.'

Faber grinned. 'His words exactly.'

'He hit Desert Wells just after we got out.'

'We?' It was Faber's turn to interupt.

Lassiter told him all that had happened. Faber gave a low whistle.

'You gonna help me find Fuller when we get to Spanish Wells?'

'Sure. I was gonna turn back when I saw the vultures takin' an interest in somethin'. I haven't seen anythin' except you for a spell. Hope you don't mind doublin' up with me.'

'Sure thing. I'm all out of walkin' fer a while.'

Faber helped him up and got into the saddle, then reached down, his hand held out for Lassiter to take.

It didn't take them long to get to Spanish Wells. Faber rode to the sheriff's office, and limped in with Lassiter following him. The sheriff of Spanish Wells was a tall man by the name of Hal Granger who had settled in Spanish Wells a while back.

'This is Rafe Lassiter, an old friend of mine,' Faber said to the sheriff.

'Good to meet you. Did you see anythin' of Hauser?'

Faber said. 'No, maybe he ain't got this far yet. Though Rafe did tell me somethin' that happened out there.' He repeated his story to Granger.

Granger shook his head. 'Don't matter too much. I've got other fellas out there. You've done all you can for now, Bill. Take it easy 'til I send for you.'

'Thanks Hal,' Faber said.

Faber took Lassiter to the small adobe house he lived in.

'You get yerself some rest, an' I'll start diggin',' he said.

'Thanks,' Lassiter replied.

When Faber had gone, Lassiter took himself to the bedroom and flopped down in the bed.

9

Dexter had come to the wagon to give Jennifer some food and water.

'Tell yer boss I got somethin' to talk to him about. Maybe we can make a deal.'

Dexter gave her a contemptuous look. 'What have you got to deal with?'

'Gold, and plenty of it,' she said, watching his face.

He gave her a suspicious look, then went out. A few minutes later he came back. Without a word, he dragged her out of the wagon, and pushed her in the direction of where Hauser was still playing with the gun.

Hauser watched her as she came. If she did know the whereabouts of the gold, it could work out pretty good for him. Get the gold, then sell her to a bordello. If there wasn't any gold he'd just sell her.

'Say what you got to say, an' make it good or I'll give you to Dexter an' the boys to play with. Savvy?'

'My husband is Jack Whelan.'

She saw Hauser become interested, and felt Dexter move behind her.

'Keep talkin',' Hauser said. 'I'll be listenin'.'

'Jack's in Spanish Wells waitin' fer me to come to him,' she said.

'Which is just what yer gonna do,' Hauser said. 'An' then what? Run off to South America with him, an' the gold?'

'Wrong,' she said sharply. 'I'm gonna kill him, an' take off with the gold.'

Hauser's eyes narrowed suspiciously. 'Why would you do a thing like that to a faithful husband that's waited fer you in a hellhole like Spanish Wells?'

''Cos he ain't bin faithful, an' he sold the rest of the gang out to the law.'

'Can't say I'm convinced,' Hauser said slowly. 'But what's yer proposition?'

'I go into Spanish Wells, go to Jack. I know just where he is. Get him to tell me where the gold is stashed. I'll put a bullet in him. We split the gold fifty-fifty, an' go our separate ways.'

'Still can't say I'm convinced. Take her back to the wagon, Dexter. Then come back here.'

'Let's go,' Dexter said.

When he had taken her to the wagon, he went straight back to Hauser.

'Reckon there's anythin' to it?' Dexter asked his boss.

'Sure there's somethin' to it. She wants the gold, an' to put a bullet in her husband. This is how we'll play it. Take her into Spanish Wells but let her go in on her own. Just you an' her an' them other two over there. Got that?'

'Sure, Link,' Dexter replied. 'I think the best thing would be to wait 'til night.'

'OK,' Hauser said.

Dexter went to the wagon.

'Yer in luck,' he told Jennifer. 'I'm gonna take you out there after dark.'

When he had gone, Jennifer felt pretty relieved. When she met up with her husband again, she'd think of a way of getting the better of them all. She had seen the way that Dexter ran his eyes over her. Maybe that was the way out.

★   ★   ★

Fuller walked to the counter where the thin woman seemed to be half dozing like she had been when he came in.

'Wuz hopin' you'd still be here,' he said to her.

Her eyes opened, and she had the look of a vulture waiting for the carcass to give up it's last breath.

'*Sí*, señor, can I be of any help?'

'A friend of mine came here awhile ago, an' I sorta lost his address,' he said. 'Jack Whelan is his name.'

'And you want me to see if I can find heem for you?' she said, sharp like a rattler's tongue.

'Catch on quick, don't you,' Fuller said with a laugh.

He fumbled in his vest pocket, and

flipped a gold coin onto the counter.

Her hand covered it like a striking scorpion.

'I weel start now, *señor*. Will there be a name?'

Fuller grinned. 'No. I want it to be a surprise.'

She gave him a knowing look, pulled the black shawl round her shoulders, and hurried into the dusty street. Fuller went out a few minutes later to find a *cantina*. He sat at the bar and looked round. There was hardly anybody in the place. A couple half-asleep fellas nursing warm beers, and a soiled dove in the far corner. Her interest picked up when Fuller walked in.

'Got the time, mister?' Donna, the soiled dove, asked when Fuller had sat down with a beer.

He gave her the once over. 'Sure. Why not? Just let me finish this beer.'

He finished the beer, stood up, and followed the soiled dove up the narrow stairs.

She opened the door, and waited for

Fuller to get inside.

'Pesos or dollars?' she asked him, and waited until he had got the coins out before starting to undress.

'Don't I know you from somewhere?' she said suddenly.

Fuller gave her a quick glance.

'Don't think so honey,' he said, getting ready.

They got into the rickety brass bed, and began to sport. As they did, Fuller saw the scar on her breast that ran from her throat to her shoulder, and it came racing to him where she knew him from.

If she remembered, and went to Whelan before he found him, it could be him that wound up with a bullet or a knife in his back.

He thought what to do about it as they sported.

'Yer mind ain't on this,' she said suddenly.

He stopped. She fastened her eyes on him, and screwed them up. She was starting to remember.

Suddenly, she said, 'I remember, you bastard.'

Fuller moved like a snake. Before she could say anything else, he forced her face down into the pillow, and held her head. She tried to kick at him, but he pinned her legs.

Soon the struggling stopped.

He got dressed, and made sure that he had left nothing that would identify him.

Carefully, he opened the door. There was nobody in the corridor. Pulling the door shut, he went downstairs. The same people were in the *cantina*, the same barman was on the bar, the same half-asleep customers. He walked unconcernedly through the bar and into the street.

10

Fuller had been out of the *cantina* ten minutes before Faber walked in.

'Where's Donna?' he asked the barkeep.

The man motioned upstairs.

'With a client?' Faber asked him.

The barman shook his head. 'No, I think he left a while back.'

'You don't mind if I go up then?' Faber asked him, heading for the stairs.

'Donna,' he shouted when he got to the door.

There was no answer.

After he had called again another couple of times he twisted the handle. One look told the ex-Ranger what he wanted to know.

'Git the sheriff,' he yelled at the owner of the *cantina* from the top of the stairs.

'What the hell's goin' on?' the owner howled back.

'Somebody's killed Donna,' Faber snarled at him.

Everybody in the *cantina* seemed to come to life.

Faber came down the stairs. 'Nobody leaves,' Faber shouted to them, limping across the dirty *cantina* floor, his hand on the butt of his .45.

He let the owner past, and then stood between everybody else and the door.

After a while the sheriff arrived with the owner of the *cantina*.

'Where is she, Bill?' he demanded.

The two of them, followed by the owner, ran up the stairs to the bedroom.

'See anybody come out?' the sheriff asked the *cantina* owner.

'Hell no. I just own this place. I ain't responsible for everythin' that goes on here.'

The sheriff came down.

'Anybody see anythin' or hear anythin' goin' on?'

Nobody said anything. The sheriff gave them a disappointed look.

'OK, Bill,' he said. 'Let's get outta here an' see if anybody else knows anythin'.'

There weren't many people out on the street, and those that the sheriff spoke to hadn't seen anything. He and Faber walked back to the *cantina* and went through the room, but found nothing.

'Seems like she upset somebody an' they just took pot luck,' the sheriff said when they had done.

Faber agreed with him, and they walked back to the office together. Lassiter was waiting for them when they got there.

'People are talkin' about a killin',' he said.

Faber told him what had happened.

'We'd better make a start tryin' to find this fella you want,' Faber said.

Lassiter agreed with him, and they walked out into the street. They walked towards the *cantina*.

'There's a couple of places along here,' Faber said as they approached the

115

boarding house that Fuller had taken a room in. Faber went in first. The thin woman was sat at the counter.

'We're lookin' fer a fella. Got in from the Cauldron. We need to talk to him,' Faber started by saying.

The woman looked at him. 'The only *hombre* that is in here today, ees the *hombre* who came in from Mexico yesterday.'

Lassiter watched her face. It was straight, with no expression on it.

'If anybody should come in you tell the sheriff right away. This *hombre* is very dangerous. *Comprende?*'

'*Sí, comprende,*' she answered.

Lassiter looked at her again. It was like she was expecting them.

'OK. *Gracias,*' he said, and went out followed by Faber.

'She's lyin',' he said when they got outside.

'They're always lyin',' Faber said. 'Learned that down on the Panhandle. It's part of their life, especially to gringos like us. We'll keep an eye on the place. I'll go first tonight. You come by around twelve. An' I'll pick it up around six. That OK with you?'

'Fine. I'll go an' get some sleep. Lend me yer key.'

Faber turned the key over to Lassiter, and watched him go back to his house.

The thin woman went to Fuller's room when Lassiter had left. She knocked on the door.

'*Sí*,' Fuller said. When she opened it and went in Fuller was lying on the bed, his hand under the cover, holding his .45.

'Yeah, what is it?'

'The man you were asking about, Whelan. He is hiding in a cabin outside the town. He is alone. Two men have been asking for you. One I know. Ees name is Faber. He walks . . . ' She searched for the word, 'With a twisted leg. The other I do not know. Thees Faber, he waits outside. I theenk ee is watching for you.'

'*Gracias, señorita*. There will be something extra for you when I leave,'

117

he said to her. 'I'll go an' see Faber before I go an' see Whelan; I've got some business to attend to with Whelan.'

'*Gracias*,' the thin woman replied, wondering if there was a reward on his head.

When she had gone, Fuller got up from the bed, and went over to his saddlebag. Feeling round inside it, he found the bone-handled knife and took it out. He tested its edge on his thumb. It needed some sharpening. He tossed it on the bed, and found a whet stone in the bag. For a while, he sharpened it up, then ran it along his thumb. It felt just fine.

He lay down on the bed, and dreamed of slitting Whelan's throat.

★ ★ ★

Jennifer and her three companions stopped on a rise overlooking Spanish Wells.

'It's down there about a mile outside

town,' she told Dexter.

'OK. I'll come in with you. Make sure he doesn't try anythin'.'

She knew exactly what he meant. He didn't trust her, and neither did Hauser. Harmon and Fielding waited in the rocks.

'OK,' she said, and gigged her horse down the slope with Dexter following her.

Whelan was sitting drinking redeye when he heard the sound of horses outside.

Draining the contents of the glass, he took out his .45, and blew out one of the two lamps. He moved to the back of the cabin, so that he had a better view of the front door. He heard the footsteps approaching the door, followed by a knock.

'Come in real slow, with yer hands up. I'll have you covered.'

The door opened and Jennifer came in, her hands above her head.

'Nice to see you ain't changed,' she said.

Whelan kept his eyes on the door, and his finger on the trigger of the .45.

'Tell yer friend to keep his hands where I can see them. One move I don't like, an' he gets it. You alone with him?'

'Hi, honey. I've just come to help you get out of this mess,' she said.

'Yeah an' what's he come to do? Help you bury me,' Whelan snarled at Dexter.

'Naw, I've come to make sure you collect what's rightfully yours. Just happened to fall in with your good lady when she was about to be caught by that bastard, Link Hauser,' Dexter lied smoothly, taking care to keep his hands where Whelan could see them.

'Just how did you come to do that?' Whelan asked Dexter.

Dexter shrugged. 'Lady had her horse shot from under her, an' I just happened to be there to pick her up, an' shoot a couple of Hauser's fellas. Ain't that right?'

'That's right,' Jennifer said. 'Jack, if it

hadn't been for him, I wouldn't be here. He deserves better than what yer givin' him.'

Whelan watched her face.

'Maybe yer right,' he said, watching the flame in the lamp go down. 'Dexter, if you want to do somethin' useful, put a lucifer to that lamp, so I can get a better gander at yer face. It's on the shelf by the door.'

Dexter took a lucifer out of his pocket and scratched it until the light flared.

'You've got as dishonest a mug as I have,' Whelan said, with a crooked grin.

'Thanks fer nothin',' Dexter said, ungratefully.

Whelan laughed. 'Just the kinda fella I like.'

'Don't want to hurry you, Jack,' Jennifer said in as sweet a voice as she could muster.

'Why?' Whelan was straightaway suspicious. 'Just what have you in mind?'

'Nothin', Jack. Just that we've got

places to go, an' — ' she stopped.

'An' what?'

'Jim Fuller's outta prison. Got to Stirlin'. Now he's come here.' Whelan half rose from the chair, and cocked the gun again. Dexter's hand dropped to his own iron, but he stopped himself from drawing it.

'Where?' a frightened Whelan demanded, his gaze running round the cabin, like a frightened rabbit.

'Should be in Spanish Wells about now,' Jennifer said quickly.

Whelan put his gun away, and licked his lips. 'We gotta get outta here.'

Jennifer looked at Dexter. 'We'd be better stayin' here,' she said.

Whelan glanced quickly at her again. 'Why do you say that?'

'We know he's comin' here. He's outgunned. I'll wait in here. Dexter'll be outside. It should be a cinch. Can you hear anythin' out there?' she asked Dexter.

'No, I can't,' Dexter said.

'Fine. Git out there, an' git yerself in

them bushes near the privy. Let him come to the cabin, then when he gets here, we'll plug him from the front, you git him in the back. Better take yer horse round the back.'

Dexter grinned like a wolf, and went outside.

* * *

Fuller had cleared the town, and was taking his time getting out to the cabin.

He had to be careful, he wasn't sure what had happened to Jennifer, and the fella who had brought her into the Cauldron. For all he knew, they might have got to Spanish Wells, she might have told him the story, and cut him in for a piece of it. He was pretty sure she was going to cut her husband out of it.

He hauled on the leathers by the dried out riverbed that the thin woman had told him about. Fuller looked round. The night was quiet. Taking the leather thong from over the hammer of his gun, he loosened it in the holster, and started towards the bend in the trail, that would bring him within sight of the Whelan's cabin.

Stopping, Fuller crouched beside the trail. He could see the cabin, with one horse tethered to the hitch rail. It looked like Jennifer had made it after all. There was nobody else who would be out here, he figured, now that Trantor's bones were somewhere in the Cauldron, along with the other fella's.

Fuller started towards the cabin, his hand resting on the butt of his gun.

A coyote sounded off to his right, somewhere out in the desert. It made Fuller jumpy, and his hands closed round the butt of his six-gun. For a split second it was halfway out of the leather.

He went on cautiously, listening. He had been going to go to the front door and just go in, but the sound of the coyote made him edgy. Moving along the side of the cabin, he stopped at the corner, and peered round. Dexter's horse was standing quietly near the bushes by the privy. He waited for a moment. To his right, stood another stand of bushes, and beyond that another stand.

Somebody, he figured was waiting to put a bullet in him.

A cloud slipped across the moon, and Fuller moved quickly to the cover of the bushes. Once in the cover, he looked towards the cabin, and the privy. The horse moved, nickering as it did so. The cloud cleared the moon, and he saw the figure of a man put his hand across the animal's muzzle to quieten it.

Fuller went for the second set of bushes, hoping that the horse had distracted the fella for long enough. There was no commotion from the bushes. It didn't take long for him to cross the ground, and come up behind the privy. There was a movement, and he saw the fella move again. Putting his gun away, he took out the knife he had killed Faber with, and crept towards the fella. When he was almost there, Dexter turned. Fuller sprang at him, his hand closing over Dexter's mouth, the knife slicing up into his belly. Twisting the knife, Fuller held on to Dexter until he had stopped squirming, then he lowered him to the ground.

11

Lassiter came looking for Faber, and found his body in the shop doorway where Fuller had left it after he had killed him. He glanced up and down the empty street, and saw the light shining from the boarding house. He knew right off that was where he should start looking.

When he opened the door, the thin woman watched his face.

'Where is he?' he demanded.

'He ees not here,' she said, as Lassiter's hands grabbed her by the front of the dress.

'Then where is he?' Lassiter pulled her clear of the floor.

'I have given eem directions to where Jack Whelan is,' she gabbled.

'An' where would that be?' Lassiter asked her, easing his grip now that she had decided to be helpful.

'Down by the dried-out riverbed,' she told him. 'Where it ees quiet.'

'Git the sheriff, an' tell him that there's a dead body across the street.'

Lassiter went to the livery stable where he had left Faber's horse. He rode out in the direction of the cabin.

★ ★ ★

Fuller stepped in the direction of the cabin, his .45 in his hand. As he got there, he saw a rear door. Bending, he listened. The sound of two voices came out through the wood.

'Takin' his damn time,' Whelan said.

'Fuller was always a man to take his own time,' Jennifer said, as the door burst open.

'Hi, Jennifer. Thought you might have saved me the price of a bullet,' he said, looking at Whelan and swinging his gun to cover each of them in turn.

'Christ, Fuller,' Whelan said, his voice shaking with fear.

'Not the man you used to be,' Fuller

said, going over to the chair Whelan was sitting in. 'Back off a mite, Jennifer.'

Jennifer stepped away from Whelan, her hand slipping to the back of her trousers, where she had secreted the gun she was carrying, not trusting Dexter.

'Git that hand where I can see it,' Fuller told her. 'I might just shoot you an' then get what I want out of yer husband.'

'For God's sake, Jim, I was gonna see you got yer share,' Whelan said from the chair.

'An' when was that going to be?' Fuller asked, bringing the gun across Whelan's nose.

Whelan screamed and brought his hands up to protect his face.

'Cut it out, Fuller,' Whelan howled as his nose bled through his fingers.

'You can put an end to it, if you want,' Fuller said. 'Just tell me where the gold is. It ain't like I was stealin'. Part of it's mine.'

'You ain't gettin' one red cent of it,'

Whelan said, trying to stop his nose bleeding.

'Sit still, or I'll shoot you, gold or no gold,' Fuller snarled, making to hit Whelan again with the butt of his gun.

Whelan put his hands up again to protect himself. Fuller's mind was set on pistol whipping him. Jennifer took the gun out of the band of her trousers and shot Fuller in the back. The force of the piece of lead flung him across Whelan and they ended up in a heap on the floor.

Jennifer put the gun away and pulled Fuller out of the way.

'You gonna tell me where that gold is?' she said, pushing the gun into her husband's chest.

'An' if I don't?' he asked.

Jennifer took a step back, raised the pistol, and shot him in the fleshy part of his arm.

Whelan screamed and Jennifer picked up Fuller's revolver. 'I reckon there's nine pieces of lead in these two guns, so you can tell me what I want to know an' end up with a broken nose, and a bloody arm, or you can have a couple in yer more sensitive parts, an' a couple in yer belly,' she said evenly.

'I worked hard to plan that robbery,' Whelan started to say.

'Save it,' came the answer as Jennifer thumbed back the hammer on her own gun.

Whelan licked his lips. 'Remember the old church a couple of miles from here?'

'Yeah. Is it in there?'

'Behind the altar. It seemed a good place to put it. A church for stolen gold. Get it?'

'I get it,' Jennifer said as she raised the pistol, and shot him.

Whelan staggered away from the table, and collapsed, blood coming out of the hole in his chest.

Jennifer stuck the gun in her waistband and stepped away from Whelan.

She stood looking at the bodies for a minute, then headed for the door.

Outside, she climbed into the saddle.

Jennifer thought about how she would get the gold out, and remembered Dexter's amigos, Fielding and Harmon. They would still be in the rocks waiting for her and Dexter.

'Who's that?' Harmon called when she got there.

'Me,' she called back.

Fielding stood behind him covering Jeniffer. He stepped from behind a rock. 'Where's Dexter?'

'Fuller got him, I got Fuller,' Jennifer said, climbing down from the saddle.

'So what about the gold?' Fielding asked her.

'Don't worry yer head about that. I know just where it is. We need a wagon. Guess that's gonna be yer boss's chore.'

'We'd better git back there, an' tell him,' Harmon said.

The three of them rode to where Hauser and his men were camped.

'We need a wagon,' Jennifer told Hauser, who was sitting in his tent getting rid of a bottle of redeye. A woman was keeping him company.

He sat up and looked at her. Hauser's eyes rolled, and the woman caught his head and twisted it round so she could kiss him.

Hauser flung her away. 'This is business.'

The woman slunk out of the tent muttering to herself.

'You know where the gold is?' he asked Jennifer.

'Sure. It's in some old church, just waitin' fer us to go an' get it,' she said, taking the bottle from Hauser. She took a long drink.

Jennifer handed it up to Fielding, who took a drink and passed it back to Hauser, who grunted. For a while Hauser said nothing, then belched loudly.

'OK, Fielding, find yerself a wagon, an' go pick the gold up. D'you need some men?'

Fielding looked at Jennifer who shook her head.

'Nah, I figure we can manage,' he

said, taking the bottle from Hauser and downing a fair mouthful.

'Go make us rich,' Hauser said, falling back onto the floor.

Jennifer and Fielding left to find a wagon. Fielding found a wagon that had been used to haul the loot out of Desert Wells. He hitched the team to it, and climbed up onto the driver's box.

'Ready?' he said to Jennifer.

She had climbed up beside him and Fielding put the leathers across the backs of the team. There was a jerk, and the wagon pulled out.

By now it was dawn, and the promise of another hot day. Fielding lashed the horses as the wagon pulled out of the canyon.

'This place, is it far?' he asked Jennifer.

'A couple of miles,' she said, watching the trail up ahead.

* * *

Lassiter saw the cabin from just round the bend. He hauled on the leathers.

Outside the cabin Lassiter found a mess of tracks. For a minute he looked at them. He walked back to where he had hitched his horse and got into the saddle. Lassiter figured that one of the sets of tracks belonged to Jennifer. He followed them up into the foothills where he found the place where she had met up with Fielding and Harmon.

He tracked them to a rise, where he dismounted and climbed to the top.

Peering down, he saw Hauser's men loafing about in the sun. He recognized Hauser, who was telling his men about the merits of the Gatling they had got hold of. There was no sign of Jennifer.

If she was looking for the gold, he figured she had got to be around somewhere.

If he went into the camp and asked Hauser, he would get a bullet.

Lassiter looked in the direction of the Gatling, which Hauser was pointing to with obvious pleasure. Behind the Gatling he saw another set of tracks where a wagon and team had been parked up. The wagon had been drawn out of the space. The tracks led out of the camp.

Lassiter returned to the bottom of the rise, and mounted up. Patiently he guided his horse round the renegade's camp until he saw where the wagon had come out. He picked up the tracks, and went after it.

★　★　★

Galloway and Gillespie had made it across the Cauldron, and were in Spanish Wells.

'Where do we start lookin'?' Galloway asked his partner.

'*Cantina* down the street seems it's the place to start. Seems to be a lot of activity out there.' Gillespie told him.

They had left their horses in the livery.

'What's all the activity?' Galloway asked the *cantina* owner.

The man shrugged his shoulders. 'One of the girls got herself killed yesterday. So everybody has come to see where it happened. People,' he said in disgust.

'Two beers,' Galloway said, tossing the coins on the wet counter-top.

The fella served them up.

'You look as though you have come a long way,' the barkeep said.

'Across the Cauldron,' Galloway told him, taking a long drink of the beer.

'Hell of a place to cross,' the owner of the *cantina* said.

'Shame about yer girl,' Galloway said, taking a drink from his own glass.

'Uh — Donna, yeah, sure. She was good at what she did. No reason that I can see for some fella suffocatin' her like that,' the fella went on.

'Any idea who done it?' Galloway asked.

'No, the fella was in and out before anybody got a look at him. Funny thing though,' the barkeep continued, 'Spanish Wells is a quiet kinda place, then we get two killin's in one day.'

The two men on the other side of the

bar exchanged glances.

'He was an ol' Texas Ranger, name of Faber, Bill Faber. Found him in a shop doorway down the block, opposite the boarding house.'

Galloway lifted his glass and drained it. 'Thanks, friend, we got to be goin'.'

★ ★ ★

'Don't know about the soiled dove up there,' Gillespie said. 'That suffocatin' sure smells of Fuller.'

'We'd best get to that boardin' house, an' see what we can see,' Galloway said.

They found the shop, and the boarding house almost dead opposite.

'The fella, Bill Faber, he was an amigo of ours,' Galloway said to the thin woman. 'You any idea who might have done it?'

'An' eef I know, how much is it worth? The law and someone else was looking for heem.'

'Who was this someone else?' Galloway asked her.

'I don't know, but like the *hombre* you are askin' about. I think he came out of the desert.'

The two men looked at her.

'Ee was asking about a friend also,' she said. 'Someone called Whelan. They were friends. So ee said.'

'You can gamble on them not bein' friends,' Galloway laughed. 'Do you know where this fella Whelan is?'

'I made it my business to. The *hombre* paid well.' She smiled knowingly.

Galloway reached for his billfold, and peeled off some notes.

'Better than that,' she said.

Galloway peeled off more notes and laid them on the counter, with his hand over them.

She smiled at Galloway. 'Yes, ee was that generous,' she said, and reached out for the money, but Galloway's hand stayed where it was.

'Ain't we forgettin' somethin'?' he asked her.

Quickly, she told him where Whelan's cabin was.

'*Adios*,' Galloway said as they left.

The woman picked up the notes, and put them away. When she had made sure they had gone, she put on her shawl and went to see the sheriff.

'I heard thees man talking,' she said to him. 'I think they were looking for the *hombre* who is using the cabin outside town. Do you know where I mean?'

'Out near the river? Sure I know where you mean,' Hal replied.

'Maybe they had somethin' to do with those two murders,' she added as sweetly as she could.

'I'll round up some men,' the sheriff told her.

The posse started out after Galloway and Gillespie not long after.

★　★　★

'That's the place up ahead,' Jennifer said to Fielding.

The walls of the place had crumbled so that you could walk in without using

140

the door. The sunlight flooded in through the breaks in the wall.

Fielding climbed down, and fastened the leathers to the brake. Jennifer was already climbing over the crumbling masonry and getting into the church. She walked up the aisle followed by Fielding. The altar rail had gone, like the walls. For a second, she hesitated, then walked up to the altar, and round to the back with Fielding still following her. Round the back of the altar it was dark, and dusty.

She stopped when she stubbed her foot against a wooden box. Fielding watched as she bent, and brushed the dust off the box.

'This is it,' she cried excitedly. 'Give me a hand.'

Fielding went round the other side of the box, and put his hands underneath it. Together they lifted it, and staggered to the front of the altar.

Both of them were gasping with the weight of the box and the heat.

'Let's get it open,' Jennifer cried as he

started to pull at the top of the box.

'That won't do any good,' Fielding said. 'We need an iron bar or somethin'.'

'Take a look round see if you can see anythin',' she told him.

Fielding walked out among the pews until he found a length of metal.

He looked at it. 'Dunno what this is doin' here,' he said.

'Provided by the good Lord,' Jennifer said with a smirk, as she took the length of metal off him.

She put the end of the metal in under the lid of the box, and brought her weight down on it. She tried a couple of times, while Fielding looked on.

'Let me at it,' Fielding said, as he watched her panting.

She stepped away from the box, and dropped the metal. Fielding picked it up, and got to work on the box.

Jennifer had sat on the step below the altar, and was wiping the sweat off her face when she heard the wood splintering and Fielding give out a yell of satisfaction.

She turned round and ran to where Fielding was wrestling something out of the box. She watched as his eyes lit up, and he took a bright, new shining bar of gold out of the box.

'Glory days,' he howled as he raised the yellow bar above his head.

Jennifer was on her knees scrabbling at the inside of the box. 'Another one,' she yelled.

Fielding put the gold bar down, and helped her to get the rest of the bars out. There were ten in all.

'We got ourselves a fortune,' Fielding laughed.

Jennifer watched him, but said nothing.

'Ol' Link's gonna be real pleased,' he laughed. 'Real pleased.'

'He'll be even more pleased when we get this stuff to him. Wanna give me a hand gettin' it in the box?'

'Sure, why not?' Fielding said.

'Yeah, why not?' Lassiter said.

His voice took them by surprise.

'Who's this fella?' Fielding asked her.

'Bounty hunter, goes by the name of Rafe Lassiter,' Jennifer replied.

Both of them raised their hands.

'Guess you're gonna put that gold in that box again,' Lassiter said easily, a smile on his lips. 'Don't let me be the one to put a stop to it. Let's keep it goin',' Lassiter told them.

The bounty hunter watched as they put the bars of gold in the box. They were both sweating, and Jennifer looked like she wanted to kill Lassiter.

When they had finished, Lassiter had them carry it outside, and put it on the wagon.

Part way to town, they almost collided head on into Galloway and Gillespie. Both men veered off the trail.

'Who the hell wuz them two? Fielding whispered to Jennifer.

Lassiter was in the back, keeping an eye on his horse, which was tethered to the wagon.

Jennifer leaned over to him. 'A couple of my husband's gang. They must be after the gold as well.'

Fielding glanced over his shoulder to make sure that Lassiter hadn't overheard them.

Ten minutes later they ran into the posse.

'What you got there?' Hal asked Lassiter when they had stopped the wagon.

'Some gold the railway's bin missin' fer a spell. An' this fella's a friend of Link Hauser who ain't a million miles from here,' Lassiter told him. 'An' two fellas that were in the gang seemed like they were headin' fer the ol' church.'

'Link Hauser?' Hal said sharply. 'Captain Stranks passed through here a couple of days ago. Got a tip Hauser was headin' up to Spanish Wells. Told us to keep a look out fer that snake. I'd better send somebody to go an' find him. He's not that far away. If he wants Hauser, he's gonna come an' get him.'

Hal looked round him. 'You two boys, go an' find Stranks and tell him to get back to Spanish Wells. Hauser's on his way here,' Hal shouted to a couple of fellas in the posse.

The two men hauled on the leathers, and headed out.

'We'll get the gold to Spanish Wells, an' lock it in the safe in the bank until we can git the railway to come an' pick it up,' Hal said. 'I'll send a couple of these boys back with you.'

He took the rest of the posse after Galloway and Gillespie.

It didn't take long to get the gold locked up in the bank, and Jennifer and Fielding behind bars.

'I guess there's a reward on that gold,' Lassiter said when he and Hal had taken a couple of bottles of beer from the saloon over to the jail.

'A fair-sized reward,' Hal said, wiping his lips off with the back of his hand. 'Galloway an' Gillespie tried to make a fight of it, so we had to bring them in over their saddles.'

They were both silent, until Hal said, 'I'll go an' see if Jennifer can help us about anythin' else.'

Lassiter took a pull of the beer, and

thought about Jim Crowe, and Ned Butler, and reminded himself once they got this mess sorted out, he'd go to Desert Wells, and buy them both the biggest headstones he could afford.

★   ★   ★

'The girl says that them two fellas are called Gillespie and Galloway. They broke out of jail along with Fuller,' Hal said when he came back.

'I found Fuller out at Trantor's place. Figure she shot him. She says them three busted outta prison. Then had some sorta fall out, an' somebody, most likely Fuller, found Stirling an' per-suaded him to tell them where Whelan was. I think we'd better get this town ready fer a fight. Hauser's gonna be along here before too long, an' he's gonna be lookin' fer trouble,' Lassiter said, reaching for another bottle.

Hal drained his bottle. 'Yer right. Just stay here, I'll get things movin'.'

The sheriff went out into the street.

147

He grabbed everybody he could get hold of.

'Git some flat-bed wagons, an' block off the main street,' he said to the mayor.

'What's got into you, Hal?' Elias Gaines, the mayor, demanded when Hal cornered him outside the general store.

'Link Hauser's gonna come callin' is what's got into me,' Hal said.

Elias Gaines' fleshy face drained of its colour when he heard this. 'We'd best be doin'.'

Hal crossed the street to the saloon where the posse had gone to clean the dust out of their throats.

'Listen up, fellas,' Hal shouted. 'Got some bad news fer you.'

The members of the posse turned in Hal's direction. 'Link Hauser's on his way here.'

The posse let out a collective groan.

'Get out into the street, an' get started making the town look like it's gonna be hard to take, and it'll cost

Hauser some of his men when he comes to try to take it.'

* * *

Harmon watched the proceedings with interest at what was going on.

Lassiter and the posse had collided before he could get Fielding out of the mess he was in. He had followed them to Spanish Wells, and decided to stay until he could figure what to do. When the town was getting ready to greet Hauser, he knew what to do. Unhitching his horse from outside the saloon, he got into the saddle, and headed to the camp.

Hauser greeted him cordially when he got there. 'Glad to see you, Harmon. Where's Dexter, an' the girl?'

'I saw them get the gold then some fella got them. They ain't comin',' Harmon said when he had got down from his saddle.

Hauser gave him a hard look. 'What d'you mean?'

The renegade told him what had happened.

Hauser swore, and took the bottle of redeye off the wagon and took a long drink.

'This is what yer gonna do,' he said. 'There's some fuse an' dynamite in the wagon. Git it, an' get to Spanish Wells. Fix yerself up near them barricades you've bin tellin' me about. When we're about to hit them, toss a couple of sticks in, an' blow that barricade so far apart that we can drive this wagon with the Gatling on, along with the men in front of it. Shouldn't take too long once the dynamite goes off. Don't worry about a signal nor nothin'. Just fix yerself up near the trail at the edge of town. Now git there, before they put anybody on the trail to see who's comin' an' goin'.'

Harmon got aboard his horse and headed in the direction of Spanish Wells.

Just after he got there Hal started sending men out to check that the trail was clear.

Harmon went into the saloon for a beer, figuring that Link and the boys wouldn't be just behind him. The barkeep came and took his order. Harmon listened to the conversation of a couple of townsfolk.

'This fella Lassiter, he brought the gold in, an' the sheriff got it stashed in the bank. Brought a couple of others in with him as well. Don't know their names, but the fella looks a bad 'un. The woman, she's pretty.'

The barkeep came back with his beer. Harmon lifted it from the counter, and took the head off. He had wondered where Fielding had got to; now he knew.

There was a chance of getting him out.

Finishing his beer, he went outside. The two sticks of dynamite and fuse were in his saddlebag. Being sure he could not be seen, he took them out of the saddlebag, and put them in his shirt.

Harmon watched the men at the top

of the street, and listened. To him the time seemed to drag, then he heard the sound of the wagon carrying the Gatling and the outriders shouting and firing into the air.

The men at the barricade put their guns to the ready, and started to fire.

Harmon had moved just into the street, and took a stick of dynamite out of his shirt. With a stogie, he lit the fuse, watched it burn for a second then tossed it to the barricade. The stick of dynamite curved as it travelled through the air. One of the men at the barricade saw it land. He raised a shout to warn the others, but the explosion cut off the shout. It flung him into the air, and tossed him away like a leaf in a storm. The wagons were torn apart, shredding those on either side.

Harmon ran to the other end of the street, and tossed the second stick among the defenders and the barricade of wagons. The effect was the same. A hole was blown in the middle of the barricade.

Harmon hauled out his gun, and ran across to the sheriff's office. As he kicked the door open and ran inside, he heard the chatter of the Gatling, and the fire from the six-guns and Winchesters as the fight was joined.

He opened the door that led to the cells, and ran along the dusty corridor.

'Where the hell have you bin?' Fielding shouted as Harmon reached his cell.

'I'm here, ain't I?' Harmon yelled, shooting the lock off the cell door. 'C'mon, we ain't got all day.'

'An' I sure ain't stayin' here on my own,' Jennifer called from the next cell.

'Git her out,' Fielding said as he came out of the cell.

Harmon shot the lock off the door, and Jennifer came out. In the office Fielding had found his rig and was buckling it on.

'OK, let's see how Link's gettin' on,' he said, opening the door.

A hunk of lead splintered the door-post above Fielding's head. He moved back inside real quick.

Lassiter had fired from the saloon. When the shooting had started, he had been upstairs with one of the soiled doves.

'Hey,' she had yelled. 'You ain't paid.'

'I ain't had my money's worth,' Lassiter called to her, fastening on his rig and looking out of the window. He had seen Harmon toss the second stick of dynamite and head in the direction of the jail, as Hauser came barrelling along the street, standing in the back of the wagon cranking the firing handle of the Gatling for all he was worth, his shoulder-length yellow hair streaming out behind him.

At the bottom of the stairs, Lassiter barged his way through a mob of panic-stricken drinkers and soiled doves until he got to the batwing doors. From there he could see the mêlée going on in the street. Between the galloping horsemen, he saw Harmon open the door. Lassiter tossed a shot in his direction, and saw a piece of wood come out of the door-frame.

Harmon ducked back inside the sheriff's office. The glass in the sheriff's window burst open, and Fielding pushed out a Winchester and started throwing lead at the bounty hunter. Lassiter fired back through the heap of renegades milling about on the street.

Hauser had the wagon carrying the Gatling ridden down to the bank.

'Git it turned round,' he hollered to the driver, so that the business end was pointing to the bank. The gun burst into life as he cranked the handle. The slugs hit the door spitting the glass inwards, and shredding the frame of the door.

'Git in there, an' get that gold outta that safe,' he yelled to Ralston and two others who were on the wagon.

Ralston jumped down, and headed for the door. He kicked the wood out of the way and ran inside, followed by the other two.

Hauser had the wagon driven along the street, firing at anybody who looked like giving him an argument. The street was pretty well cleared when he got to the end. He had the wagon turned round, and headed back the way he had come.

'You got him pegged?' Harmon asked Fielding as he looked though the broken glass of the sheriff's office.

'In the saloon across the street,' came the reply.

'Git out the back an' git Hauser over here. Tell him this fella's gonna give us some trouble unless we get him outta there.'

Fielding went through the sheriff's office and out the back, through the alleys that led from the office.

'How are you doin', sweet thing?' Harmon asked Jennifer when she crawled through from the cells.

'Wuz doin' fine 'til he opened up on us,' she said.

'He won't be doin' that fer long, just 'til Link gets here with that gun,' Harmon said.

Lassiter watched the street from the saloon. Most of the firing had died away, there was just some coming from the edge of town. After a few minutes he heard a wagon coming into the street. Hauser had it pulled up outside the saloon, the business end of the gun facing the saloon. Lassiter didn't stick around to see what happened when Hauser started to crank the handle.

He crawled across the floor and got out to the back just as the first burst from the Gatling started to chew the place up.

He ran across the yard and out into the alley at the same time as two of Hauser's men came into the back of a shop. The two men barely had time to register Lassiter before he cut them down. The bounty hunter stepped over the bodies, and ran towards the rail where he had hitched his horse. The ground was ploughed up by pieces of lead as he climbed into the saddle. A couple of pieces plucked at his shirt as he rowelled the horse out of town.

Some of Hauser's men started to run for their horses, but Hauser, who had jumped off the wagon, yelled at them to let Lassiter go.

'He ain't gonna be no trouble.'

Lassiter rode hard until he was out of town, and reined in on a bluff overlooking the trail out of Spanish Wells.

Below him he could see some of the buildings burning, shimmering as they burned, tall plumes of black smoke reaching into the sky. The town had been ringed by Hauser's renegades and he could see them taking the gold out of the bank.

When they had finished, Hauser climbed into the rear of the wagon and yelled to the driver. The horses twitched and the wagon pulled out, heading in the direction of the border. As it drew out, Lassiter saw the reward from the gold getting away. The thought riled him. To have come all this way for nothing. Lassiter spat, and rowelled the horse down the shallow slope after the wagon.

He kept a good distance between himself and the renegades. The wagon was throwing up a heap of dust, and was surrounded by forty or so renegades. As they rode on, he wondered what had become of Jennifer. Maybe she was in the wagon with the gold. The last thing she would want was to be separated from the gold. She'd get her share any way she could, he figured.

Night had started to fall. The renegades, along with the wagon, pulled off the trail. Lassiter pulled off after them, and waited as they set up their camp. A few fires were lit and Lassiter crawled through the undergrowth, so that he could get some idea of what they were up to. Food and redeye started getting passed round the fire.

As it was being passed round, Link Hauser came out of the wagon, followed by Jennifer. She had her hair tied behind her head and was wearing a low-cut blouse with a Mexican pattern on it. Both of them were laughing and looking real friendly. Lassiter guessed why they were late coming to get some food. Any idea of any help from that side of the fence was burning up like some of the grub.

Quietly, the bounty hunter crawled away to think about things.

As the night wore on, the noise from the renegades got louder, and Lassiter figured the redeye was taking a beating. The camp had been made in a clearing about half a mile off the trail.

With the first flickering of dawn, the camp had fallen silent.

Time to go, he figured. Slowly he got up and caught hold of his horse's leathers, and led him down to the camp. It was like he figured. The redeye had put them all to sleep.

Cautiously, he stepped over the sleeping bodies. A couple of times one of them stirred in his drunken sleep and Lassiter got ready to use his knife.

Hauser's wagon, holding the gold and the Gatling, was right in the middle of the snoring men. Lassiter hitched his horse to the rear and climbed up inside.

The woman's scent caught his

nostrils as he got in there, and he felt the coldness of a gun at the side of his head.

'Hold it, Lassiter,' she whispered. 'This is my gold, so why don't you just climb right on out of here?'

'Wrong. This gold belongs to the railway company you an' yer husband stole it off.'

He heard the gun being cocked.

'You'd have a hard time explaining to Hauser what yer doin' in here with his gold, a gun, an' me,' he said.

He felt her relax and uncock the gun. 'Guess yer right. I've hitched the team up. I'll drive, you operate that gun, if you can, an' we'll get out of here.'

'OK,' Lassiter said. 'But as soon as we're out of here, this gold goes back to the people who own in.'

'We split the reward. I ain't slept with Hauser just fer the fun of it.'

'Fine, but let's get out of here,' Lassiter said.

Jennifer crawled to the seat and took hold of the leathers.

Behind her, Lassiter started to load the Gatling.

Suddenly, the wagon bounced and lurched. There were a couple of screams, as some of Hauser's men got their head stove in by the wheels.

In the last couple of minutes the sun had come up. Lassiter sent a stream of lead into the renegades as the wagon took off.

Up ahead of him he heard the snap of a bull-whip and the shouts of Jennifer.

Back at the camp, Hauser's men were pulling themselves together.

'C'mon, you lazy bastards,' Hauser yelled above the mayhem.

Finding his horse, he saddled it, and glowered down from the saddle as the camp started to sort itself out.

The wagon bounced out of the clearing and out onto the trail. In the back Lassiter waited until the renegades started showing themselves.

He didn't have that long to wait. The first of them came, galloping out of the clearing and onto the trail, enraged by the theft of the gold. Lassiter sent a long stream of fire from the Gatling into them.

Hauser, who was out front, had a lucky escape, the hot lead just missing him and taking down the fella next to him.

Some of the renegades had their carbines out and were sending some lead back at Lassiter.

Lassiter felt the hot lead grazing his arm, he yelled angrily, and fed more lead into the renegades.

Saddles were empting pretty fast now, and Hauser was getting worried. Finally, he hauled on his leathers, and pulled to the side of the trail.

'We givin' up, Link?' Ralston called out to him.

'No, goddam it, we ain't givin' up unless you want to ride into the mouth of that Gatling. They got to be headin' somewhere. We just gotta find out where.'

Lassiter eased his hand over the muzzle of the Gatling. It was starting to get real hot. He looked out of the back of the wagon.

'You can ease off a mite. Looks like they've given up.'

He felt the wagon start to slow down as Jennifer hauled on the leathers and kicked on the brake.

'Lucky to get away with that,' she said breathlessly as she climbed into the back of the wagon.

'Yeah. That Gatling was gettin' real hot,' he said.

Jennifer leaned over him and took off his bandana. 'I'm just gonna fasten up yer arm,' she said.

'Any idea where we're goin?' she asked him.

'Sorta.'

'What do you mean, 'sorta'?' Jennifer asked him.

'There's a tradin' post just down the trail. The fella's a pal of mine. We'll leave the gold there 'til we shake Hauser an' his boys off.'

Jennifer said nothing, but looked thoughtful.

'I'm gonna see if there's any sign of Hauser an' his boys,' Lassiter said as he

164

got down out of the wagon.

He walked back along the trail, his gun in his hand. He walked quite a ways but found nothing. Turning round he walked back to where he had left Jennifer and the wagon.

It came as the hell of a shock to realize the wagon and Jennifer were gone. Lassiter cursed himself for a fool as he followed the wagon tracks.

He sure wasn't going to make that mistake again. He started walking in the direction that the wagon had gone in, and he was never going to find them without a horse, his own still hitched to the wagon. After half an hour he gave it up. It was obvious that she was whipping the skin off the team's back.

Not too far away Hauser and his boys were thinking about giving up themselves. Hauser had figured it would be easy to find the trail of the wagon, but the grassy ground gave way to hard rocky ground and the tracks petered out.

'We're gonna have to split up boys,' he said.

Hauser sent his renegades off in different directions.

'Be back here in a couple of hours. If you see anythin' just fire a couple of shots in the air.'

The groups rode off to find the wagon and Jennifer.

★ ★ ★

Hauling on the reins, Jennifer got the wagon to a halt. It was a stupid thing to have done on the spur of the moment. She had nowhere to go, and it would take Hauser and Lassiter no time to find her.

She started to figure out what she needed. The first thing she needed was somewhere to ditch the gold and the wagon, so she could come back later. She also needed a gun. She had wanted a saddle horse, but Lassiter's was still hitched to the wagon. Jennifer got down and took a look at it. That would take her a fair ways. She needed a six-shooter or some kind of gun.

Walking to the front of the wagon, she climbed up. Lashing the team she guided it onto the trail.

For a while all she could see were rocks, and the hot sun. There was no sign of a living soul.

As the day went on she wondered if it hadn't been such a great idea, but then, she wasn't going to come out of this deal with less than she went in.

The rocks started to thin out, except for a stack that looked like a chimney.

She steered the horses in that direction. When she got there the sweat was running down her face and sticking her blouse to her body.

Swinging down she took a look round. The chimney was a couple of hundred feet high, so the gold wasn't going up there. Walking round the chimney, she found a hole that wasn't all that deep. It would do, she told herself.

Going back to the wagon, she drove

it round to the other side of the chimney and got down. The box was hemmed in between the Gatling and the driver's seat.

Climbing into the back she looked at the Gatling. That would have to stay where it was. She couldn't move the driver's seat. Hauser had left the cover on the wagon. That was the way, she told herself.

Climbing over the box of gold, Jennifer started to unfasten the hide that held the cover on the wagon. It wasn't long before the sweat was oozing out of her skin.

Her breathing coming heavily, she bent down and dragged the box holding the gold to the side of the wagon, and put it down it until she got her breath back then pulled it over the side of the wagon and let it hit the desert floor.

She stayed in the wagon breathing hard for a spell, her face masked with dust, her fingernails cracked and bleeding. Out through the side where she had taken the cover of the wagon off, she watched a mess of buzzards circling over something dead.

She hauled herself out of the wagon and dropped to the ground. Getting to her feet, she caught the smell of something acrid and burning.

'Pretty fine smell, if you like tobacco.'

She turned quickly. The fella was sitting on a rock smoking his pipe. His face was lined like an old saddle. A grin split it. Taking the pipe from his mouth he flicked it, so the spittle stained the ground.

'You seemed to be enjoyin' yerself, so I thought I'd let you alone. That all the gold?'

She looked at him sharply.

'I've bin followin' you since Desert Wells, an' you an' yer friends have led me a pretty dance,' he said, putting another lucifer to his pipe, and puffing on it.

'Just who the hell are you?' Jennifer demanded angrily. 'An' what do you want?'

'I'm a bounty hunter just tryin' to

make a livin'. Where's Rafe by the way?'

'We got separated,' Jennifer told him, wondering just where the hell the bounty hunter was.

'Best hope Hauser don't catch either of you or he'll separate yer breath from yer bodies. After he's taken his pleasure with you,' he added with a laugh.

'OK Mister Bounty Hunter, just what do you want?'

He seemed to relax a mite. 'Just want my fair share of the gold. I ain't bothered about takin' it back to them railway people.'

'How much is a fair share?' Jennifer asked him, eyeing the .45 in his hand.

He sucked in the smoke. 'Half,' he said, like he was doing her a favour.

Half, she thought. It could have been worse, he could have just taken the whole lot.

Jennifer pretended to think about the offer while she looked him up and down. She sure could use that heavy .45 he was packing, and his horse had a lot of miles in it.

'What's yer name?' she asked him.

'Hank Blackstone,' he replied, admiring her figure.

'OK, Hank Blackstone, you've got yerself a deal. But that's only the gold,' she said, seeing how he was looking at her.

'Wouldn't have it any other way,' Blackstone said, getting up from the rock and coming over to her.

'What wuz you gonna do with it?' he asked her, pointing to the box.

'Drop it in the hole, an' come back fer it later,' she told him.

'That way you wouldn't have it on you if Link caught up with you, an' the horse would give you better travellin' time. You could blame the whole thing on Rafe.'

'I'd have to keep clear of Rafe Lassiter until I was well out of that part of the country.'

'Rafe,' Blackstone mused, emptying out his pipe. 'I ain't seen him fer a spell. How's his ol' buddy Crowe?'

'Lassiter seems to think Crowe's

dead. Say, how come you know Lassiter?'

Blackstone didn't answer right off. 'Me an' him did some huntin' a while back.'

'Fer men from the way yer talkin',' Jennifer said.

'Best kinda huntin' there is,' Blackstone said with relish in his voice. 'Pity that Rafe an' me is on the same side of the law. Wouldn't mind goin' up against him.'

'I'd think twice about that,' Jennifer told him. 'He can sure as hell handle himself.'

'Yeah, that's what I mean,' Blackstone replied. 'I ain't gonna leave that gold in that hole even if I am tottin' you around with me. I ain't sure I can trust you. It's gonna have to come with us.'

Jennifer said nothing, she was just going to have to do something with him.

Blackstone was trying to figure a way to haul the gold with them and not use the wagon. Jennifer watched him closely, then started to make her way to the wagon. Inside it, just behind the Gatling, was a shovel. Reaching in she got her hands on it. Blackstone was still trying to figure what to do with the gold as she moved up quietly behind him, raising the shovel as she came.

'I figured it out,' he said, starting to turn.

Jennifer swung the shovel.

Blackstone yelled as it struck the back of his head. He folded up, and hit the dust.

When he didn't move, she reached down and pulled out the Peacemaker.

Levelling at him, she drew back the hammer. Her hand shook as she pointed it at his head. Suddenly, she lowered the gun. She just couldn't kill him like that. She was a better man than him.

She slipped the hammer and put the gun in her waistband.

12

Lassiter stood in the middle of the trail for a few minutes. Then he moved to the side. Hauser's men couldn't be too far behind him. He moved in among the rocks and thin scrub that overlooked the trail.

If Hauser had any sense, he thought, he'd split up his men so that they could cover more ground.

Taking out his .45 he checked it and put a sixth round in the last chamber, and settled himself to wait.

As the time passed and nothing happened, he thought he might be wrong.

Then he heard the cantering of horses coming down the trail. The horses stopped occasionally like somebody was checking the trail. He saw them. Three riders not paying any particular attention to anybody that might be waiting for them.

The fella that seemed to be in charge was big and heavy, carrying a brace of .45s at his hip, and taking the occasional swallow from the bottle of redeye he was passing from one of his amigos to the other.

The men were laughing drunkenly as they came along the trail.

Lassiter froze suddenly. The fella was wearing Crowe's battered old hat. Lassiter had felt all along that Crowe was dead. Now he could see the fella wearing the proof.

He stepped onto the trail in plain view of them, his .45 in his hand.

The three stopped, hauling drunkenly on the leathers of their horses.

'What the hell's this?' the one wearing Crowe's hat asked.

'Death an' damnation,' Lassiter replied, cocking his .45.

'Death an' what?' the fella demanded.

'Death an' damnation,' Lassiter said patiently, not taking his eyes off the other men.

The three men exchanged glances.

'What's he talkin' about, Jake?'

'I ain't rightly sure,' Jake said. 'But I don't think he means us any good.' Jake's hand dropped to one of the .45s, as the bottle of redeye fell out of his hand and smashed on the trail.

Lassiter fired and Jake was punched out of the saddle, bleeding but not dead.

The other two men were reaching for their pieces, but the horses, which had spooked at the sound of the first shot, were making things hard for their riders.

Giving himself some room to shoot, Lassiter had moved to the edge of the trail.

He picked the rider in buckskins, and shot him off his horse before he could clear leather. Lassiter's piece of lead took him high in the throat and he fell out of the saddle, blood bursting from the wound. Lassiter's third target had time to get off a shot that went wide before Lassiter's bullet took his life.

The lead from the third fella nicked Lassiter's cheek. Lassiter's slug kicked him out of the saddle.

Lassiter broke open his gun, and let the shells fall out onto the trail.

Behind him he could hear Jake choking.

'Where'd you git the hat?' Lassiter asked the big fella.

'Why? He a buddy of yours?' Jake asked, the blood starting to come from between his thick lips.

'Yeah,' Lassiter told him.

'He won't need any buddies where he's gone.'

Lassiter finished him off.

He checked each body to make sure that they were all dead.

One of the horses had spooked and galloped off down the trail. Lassiter gathered the leathers of the rest of the horses and mounted Jake's, the one that he reckoned to be the best, and went looking for Jennifer and the gold.

★　★　★

Jennifer stood over Blackstone, her finger close to squeezing the trigger.

She stopped and listened. A couple of horses were approaching the chimney rock from somewhere off to the left.

It was Hauser or his boys. Lassiter would still be walking.

Uncocking the pistol she put it in her waist-band and scrambled up into the saddle, and galloped away.

Lassiter reached the chimney rock a couple of minutes later with the wagon still stuck in the middle of the trail. He jumped down and took a look at the wagon.

Walking round he saw Blackstone lying in the dust. He bent over the fella.

'Hi, Hank. What hit you?' he said as Blackstone started to move.

'That damn bitch you were hooked up with,' Blackstone groaned.

'Stay here, I'll get you some water,' Lassiter said.

He came back with a canteen, and poured water on his bandanna.

'That feels a damn sight better,' he

moaned when Lassiter had cleaned off the back of his head, and fed him a drink.

He told Lassiter what happened.

'Any idea what she did with the gold?' Lassiter asked the bounty hunter.

'No,' Blackstone said, deliberately not looking at the hole.

'She can't have gone far with it,' Lassiter said. 'We can always look fer it after we've caught up with her. If Hauser doesn't git to her first.'

Lassiter bent low in his saddle. 'These are her tracks. Let's git.'

Lassiter and Blackstone rowelled their horses and started to follow the tracks.

13

'Sure I know Rafe Lassiter,' Slim Ransome said to Jennifer.

He had seen the girl riding out of the desert like she was in the hell of a hurry. He looked her up and down. She seemed genuine enough. Her clothes were covered in dust, and she looked scared.

'He wants me to give you some food, an' he'll pay when he gets here in a day or so,' he said. 'Yeah,' Jennifer said quickly.

A mite too quickly, Ransome thought.

'He's takin' some fella back across the Cauldron. One of Link Hauser's boys,' Jennifer said a little more slowly.

'I heard Hauser was in the territory,' Ransome said, resting the heavy bucket on the lip of the well.

'He hit Spanish Wells a couple of

days back, but the sheriff and his boys were ready fer him. It's about time somebody gave Hauser a whipping.'

Ransome lowered the bucket down the well and let it fill up. He was a middle-aged man who had seen more than his fair share of hard times, and heard more than his fair share of lies. While he couldn't say Jennifer was a liar, there was something about her story that rang like a bell with a crack in it.

'OK, I'll fix you up with some grub, an' some fresh clothes if you want' em.'

Jennifer couldn't believe her luck. The old fool had bought every word of her story.

'That would be just fine,' she said gratefully.

Ransome hauled up the full bucket. She followed him inside the trading post. He put the bucket on the floor under the table, and started fixing some food.

'When you've eaten yer fill,' he said

to her, 'you can go in there an' try some clothes on.

She's dead now, but I reckon yer about the same.

'I sure appreciate that,' Jennifer said, sitting at the table, and taking up the eating irons.

While she was eating, Ransome went into the back room, and pulled some clothes out of a drawer, and threw them on the bed.

'You finished eatin'? 'Cos if you have, you might as well come an' try these clothes on,' Ransome called out to her.

'Yeah, I've just about finished,' she called back.

Ransome went through to where she was eating.

'Jes' give me a call when yer ready,' he told her. 'I've got to go into the yard to sort a couple of things out.'

He waited until he heard the door close, then hurried back inside. Ransome leaned against it, and locked it.

'Hey, what d'you think yer doin'?'

Jennifer yelled when she realized that she had been locked in the room.

'Jes' makin' sure you don't go runnin' off before Rafe gets here,' he shouted through the wood. 'Yer story was just a little too convincin'.'

'Damn it, you ol' fool, let me outta here,' Jennifer yelled as she beat on the door.

'Later — when Rafe gits here.'

'Let me outta here,' she screamed at him.

'Settle yerself down. It's too damn hot fer that kinda noise,' Ransome told her.

He went out into the yard to make himself a stogie, figuring Rafe wouldn't be too long.

★   ★   ★

Hauser had come across the bodies of his men.

'Git everybody down here, then we can go after that woman,' he shouted at the top of his voice.

The riders went off in search of their amigos. It took a couple of hours to round them all up.

'OK, let's get that trail found,' Hauser told them.

A couple of his boys had already started looking for the trail.

'We got it,' one of them yelled as the rest came round a bend in the trail.

The renegades headed off in the direction of the trading post.

★   ★   ★

'There's a little lady waitin' fer you in there,' Ransome told Lassiter and Blackstone when they hauled up outside the trading post.

'Figured she'd show up here,' Lassiter said, dropping out of the saddle. 'She ain't no place else to go.'

Blackstone followed him down.

'Let's go an' see what she's got to say for herself,' Lassiter said.

Jennifer had stopped trying to break the door down. She sat on the edge of the bed waiting for Ransome.

'You still in there, Jennifer?' Lassiter shouted when he got there.

'Where the hell else would I be?' she shouted back.

'Over the hill an' far away,' Lassiter said with a laugh.

The laugh riled her.

'What's so damn funny?' she shouted back through the door.

'You're so damned funny,' Lassiter shouted to her. 'If you just tell me where you left that gold we can go our separate ways.'

There was a silence.

'Why don't you just tell me, an' save yerself some time in jail?'

Jennifer knew that if Lassiter caught up with her he'd take her in. What would Hauser do if he caught up with her? She went cold at the thought.

'OK, Lassiter, you got yerself a deal,' she told him, disconsolately.

Ransome had been watching the trail from the yard. He hurried inside.

'Don't think yer goin' no place,' he

said to Lassiter.

Blackstone looked at him and hurried outside. A couple of minutes later there was a spattering of shots.

'Get her out of there,' Lassiter told Ransome and hurried outside.

Blackstone had started to barricade the door.

'Hauser,' he told Lassiter. 'Reckon he's come fer the gold.'

'I hate to disappoint a fella when he's got his heart bent on somethin',' Lassiter replied. 'But we're gonna have to disappoint ol' Link.'

Blackstone laughed.

The shooting became more intense as more of the renegades caught up with their amigos.

'Give me a gun,' Jennifer shouted to Lassiter.

'I've got one,' Ransome said, taking one out of the drawer, and tossing it to the woman.

Hauser's men had circled the post and were throwing a torrent of lead that way.

'What we need is somethin that can really hurt them,' Lassiter said as the post started to fill up with gun smoke.

'We're gonna have to do somethin',' Jennifer said.

'Got some dynamite,' Ransome said suddenly.

Lassiter and Blackstone looked at him.

'Where?' Lassiter asked him quickly.

'See that ol' hut about halfway between them an' us?' Ransome said. 'It's in there.'

'That's where it is?' Lassiter asked Ransome.

'Yeah, that's where it is,' Ransome told him.

'A heap of use that is,' Blackstone said.

'Look,' Jennifer said.

The others took a look through the loopholes. Two of Hauser's men were coming their way holding a white flag.

'I'll go see what they want,' Lassiter said, standing up.

He handed his gun to Blackstone and opened the door.

Hauser's men looked in a pretty mean mood.

'OK,' the one with the eye patch said. 'You ain't goin' any place, so just hand over the gold, and we'll leave you in peace. We won't do you any harm, or to the woman. Though Link ain't best pleased about what she did to him.'

'It ain't just up to me,' Lassiter replied. 'There's other folks in there, an' they've got a say as well.

The two men looked at each other.

'Ten minutes,' said the one with the patch. 'Then we burn you out. Got that?'

'We got that,' Lassiter replied, a plan forming in his head.

Like hell they were going to let them go.

'Go an' see what yer boss says,' he told them, his hand moving to the back of his belt where he kept his knife.

The two men turned their backs on him and started back to where Hauser was standing. Lassiter moved like a striking snake. The knife came smoothly out of the scabbard and flashed across the intervening space like a vulture before embedding itself in the one-eyed man's back. As his amigo turned, bringing up the Winchester, Lassiter threw himself at him and brought him to the ground. His hand fastened round the fella's throat as Hauser's men began firing. A second later Blackstone, Ransome and Jennifer started firing.

One-eye's amigo wasn't too much of a challenge for Lassiter, who knew he had to be quick. As the man went limp, Lassiter disentangled himself from his legs and charged at the flimsy door of the hut.

It crashed in.

Lassiter got to his feet and looked round. There was a lot in there. Guns, ammunition, redeye, and in a corner under some covers, a case of dynamite and some fuse.

All he was short of was a box of lucifers.

Lassiter swore violently to himself. He listened to the sound of the firing. It had warmed up a mite.

He was going to have to be quick if he was going to get over to the trading post in one piece. He picked up the case and some fuse. Tucking it under his arm he opened the door and looked outside. The trading post was directly opposite. So, if he was careful he could get to the post and keep the hut between him and Hauser's men.

The lead kicked up the dust as he ran. It hadn't taken long for him to get out to the post, but it sure as hell seemed to be taking him longer to get back.

He jumped over the body of the one-eyed man, whose blood had stained the dust darkly. A bullet slammed into the corpse as he skipped over it. It kicked it up a little, just as a slug tore into his sleeve.

Lassiter glanced down at it. Another half inch and it would have blown him into the post.

As he got to the veranda, Blackstone pulled the door open, and Lassiter got inside. Blackstone slammed the door closed behind him, a heap of lead drilling holes into it.

'Glad to see you agin,' Jennifer said, as she took the dynamite and fuses off him.

'Glad to be back,' Lassiter said with a nervous laugh.

'How's about gettin' this dynamite fixed up,' Blackstone said, taking a couple of sticks out of the case and starting to cut the fuse into short lengths.

'Somethin's goin' on out there,' Ransome yelled.

Going over to the loophole Lassiter took a look outside. A couple of Hauser's men were heading their way holding lighted torches. Lassiter snatched a stick of dynamite from Blackstone and put a lucifer to it.

'When I say so,' he said to Jennifer, 'open the door and close it damn quick.'

'Anythin' you say.'

'Right,' Lassiter yelled.

Jennifer opened the door and Lassiter

stepped out onto the veranda. A hail of lead ploughed out the wall.

He threw the stick under arm and stepped back into the post.

The two men watched the stick of dynamite curling in their direction. It landed at their feet and blew them to bloody rags.

'Whew,' Blackstone yelled.

For a while there was silence, like Hauser's men had been taken by surprise and were licking their wounds.

'That should get us some time,' Lassiter said, as Jennifer passed round a bottle of Ransome's redeye.

He looked across the yard. The sun was starting to set.

'Seems like we're gonna have us some more trouble soon,' he said to the others.

'It's gonna be dark in less than an hour,' Blackstone said, checking his .45.

In the gathering gloom, Hauser was planning his next move.

'Ralston, you take a couple of these boys, an' get that wagon. Fill it up with scrub or anythin' that'll burn,' Hauser said, watching the trading post.

'What you got it mind, Link?' Ralston asked him.

'Jus' don't want them over there feelin' the cold,' Hauser said maliciously.

Ralston laughed. 'Gotcha, boss.'

He disappeared to get things organized.

★　★　★

'Somethin's goin' on out there,' Ransome said when he caught the movement in the failing light.

Lassiter came from the back room where he and Jennifer were catching some rest while things were quiet.

'Whatever it was, it's stopped now,' Blackstone said.

'What kinda look did you get at it?' Lassiter asked him.

'Not much of a look, but I think it was big, an' they were pullin' it or somethin'.'

Lassiter moved up to get a better look. A bullet whipped a piece of wood out of the post wall.

'Somebody's keepin' an eye on us,' Blackstone said with a laugh.

★ ★ ★

'It's all fixed up, boss,' Ralston said to Hauser as he squatted down beside him.

'It'll soon be full dark,' Hauser replied. 'Jus' give it another half hour or so. See if any of those big clouds cover the moon fer us.'

They settled back to wait.

'Let's git things goin',' Hauser said to Ralston.

Ralston moved away to where the wagon was. He took out a box of lucifers and lit the oil-soaked torch with one, then tossed it into the wagon. The wood and scrub in the wagon started to burn right off.

'Start pushin',' he told the men.

'C'mon, git a move on. It ain't gonna push itself over there.'

'You try pushin'. It's damned hot

back here,' one of his boys said in an aggrieved way.

Ralston hauled out his .45. 'You want to push it or d'you want to ride in it?'

*   *   *

'What the hell is that?' asked Blackstone, who had been dozing.

Ransome pushed him out of the way and looked through the loophole.

'It's the wagon we use fer haulin' supplies. That fella Hauser's gonna have to pay fer it.'

'Just start pickin' them fellas off that are pushin' it,' Lassiter shouted. 'There's enough light to do that by.'

He picked up his .45, and started firing at the men. His first piece of lead killed Ralston, who was standing by the flaming wagon to encourage the others. Jennifer, Ransome and Blackstone got involved right off. The wagon crept nearer and the burning embers were starting to fly off the wagon, helped by a growing wind.

'This ain't no good,' Lassiter said, holstering his .45 and picking up a stick of dynamite.

'That ain't gonna do any good,' Ransome hollered. 'Yer jus' gonna blow lumps of burnin' wood onto the post.'

'Can you think of anythin' better?' Lassiter asked him. 'It's a choice of burnin' or being burnt.'

The others looked at each other and shrugged. Then started to load up their pistols.

Lassiter hauled his lucifers out of his pocket, and nodded to Jennifer who opened the door.

Lassiter dashed onto the veranda with the dynamite and lit lucifer in his hand.

As he put the lucifer to the stick of dynamite, there was a crack of thunder and a steak of lightning that took everybody by surprise. A mighty torrent of rain started to fall.

Lassiter threw the stick of dynamite over the heads of the stunned renegades.

The three of them ran out into the

yard, which was rapidly turning into a quagmire. The downpour was putting out the fire on the wagon, but Hauser's men were still full of fight. A bullet tore into Ransome's arm, it's force flinging him to the mud. Lassiter and Blackstone were taking slow toll of the renegades. The hammer of Lassiter's gun fell on an empty chamber as he was confronted by Hauser, holding a shotgun.

'You bastard,' Hauser yelled, pulling back the hammers. He raised the shotgun, his finger tightening on the trigger.

Lassiter muttered, 'Sorry, Crowe.'

'Go to hell,' Hauser screamed.

The lightning forked the night sky, and hit Hauser's shotgun.

For a second he stood rigid, then burst into flames. Still screaming, he fell to the ground.

'It's OK, Rafe,' a voice cut through the rain. 'We got them.'

It took Lassiter a few seconds to realize it was Stranks, astride his horse, the rain washing the blood off his sabre, and his men finishing off the rest of the renegades.

'You want to be careful with that sabre,' Lassiter said.

'It's OK,' Stranks said, putting the sabre into the scabbard. 'The storm's played itself out.'

When he had stopped speaking there was a roll of thunder, but it was a distance off. Lassiter got to his feet. The fire in the wagon was out, and he could see soldiers herding the surviving renegades towards the trading post's corral.

'How are the others?' Lassiter asked Stranks.

'Ransome's all right, but I saw the girl from the stage and some other fella riding out that way,' he said, pointing in the direction of chimney rock.

'See you later, Stranks.' Lassiter turned and headed towards the barn where his horse was.

Blackstone and Jennifer were going after the gold.

His horse was still saddled. Pulling

the leathers off the rail, he got aboard, and rowelled it out of the barn.

He rode hard towards the chimney rock, with the sun rising and already drying out the ground.

He hauled on the leathers when he reached the ridge that looked down on the wagon. For a moment he scanned the barren area. Jennifer was sitting on the driving seat, and Blackstone was hauling something out of the hole.

Dismounting, Lassiter started to walk in that direction. As he got nearer, he kept the wagon between him and Blackstone.

'You ain't in such good condition,' he said to Blackstone. 'Knew a time when haulin' a box out of the ground wouldn't make you break sweat. Git round here, Jennifer. I got Hank covered, an' I'm faster than him.'

He heard her come round to where Blackstone had been pulling the box out of the ground.

'Didn't think you'd git here so quick, Rafe,' Blackstone said, a mite breathlessly.

'Goes to show what you can do if you

set yer mind to it,' Lassiter said.

'Sure does,' Blackstone replied. 'What say we split the gold? There's more than enough fer the three of us.'

Lassiter shook his head. 'An' spend my life dodgin' somebody like me. No thanks. There's a lot of good bounty hunters out there. You used to be one of them.'

'Still am,' Blackstone said.

Again Lassiter shook his head. 'You just crossed the line.'

'You know, Rafe, our trails ain't crossed all that often, but I reckon I'm faster than you. What about it? Winner takes all.'

'Yeah, Rafe, what about it? Think about ol' Crowe. What d'you suppose he'd say if you backed off now?'

What she said hit Lassiter. 'Maybe yer right,' he said, holstering his gun.

Blackstone rubbed his hands on the side of his trousers to get the sweat off.

The seconds ticked by as each waited for the other to make his move. Blackstone moved first.

The shot rang out, the noise rebounding off the rocks.

Blackstone staggered back clutching his heart and fell into the hole, his gun falling to the ground.

'You know, Jennifer,' Lassiter said, dropping his .45 into the leather. 'You ain't a bad sort. Maybe I could make somethin' outta you when you git outta prison. I know some well-placed folks who'll make sure you don't go to the pen fer too long.'

'Yer ain't a great lookin' fella, Lassiter,' she said, looking up at him. 'I reckon I'll think about it.'

THE END

We do hope that you have enjoyed reading this large print book.

Did you know that all of our titles are available for purchase?

We publish a wide range of high quality large print books including:
Romances, Mysteries, Classics
General Fiction
Non Fiction and Westerns

Special interest titles available in large print are:
The Little Oxford Dictionary
Music Book, Song Book
Hymn Book, Service Book

Also available from us courtesy of Oxford University Press:
Young Readers' Dictionary
(large print edition)
Young Readers' Thesaurus
(large print edition)

For further information or a free brochure, please contact us at:
Ulverscroft Large Print Books Ltd.,
The Green, Bradgate Road, Anstey,
Leicester, LE7 7FU, England.
Tel: (00 44) **0116 236 4325**
Fax: (00 44) **0116 234 0205**